Startled, Jess came to an abrupt stop as the man who had once been the center of her world stepped out of the shadows of a spruce tree. The bag of groceries slipped from her grasp, and only Scott's quick reflexes kept it from hitting the sidewalk. He moved swiftly toward her and made a successful grab for it, which salvaged the canned goods— but dented her heart. Only inches away, his tangible, physical presence drove the breath from her lungs and she stumbled backward, desperately trying to put distance between them, unable to deal with the sudden, too-close proximity.

She would recognize him anywhere. Yet he was different. And it was more than the physical changes.

Books by Irene Hannon

Love Inspired

*Home for the Holidays #6
*A Groom of Her Own #16
*A Family To Call Her Own #25
It Had To Be You #58
One Special Christmas #77
The Way Home #112
Never Say Goodbye #175

*Vows

IRENE HANNON

has been a writer for as long as she can remember. This prolific author of romance novels for both the inspirational and traditional markets began her career at age ten, when she won a story contest conducted by a national children's magazine. Today, in addition to penning her heartwarming stories of love and faith, Irene keeps quite busy with her "day job" in corporate communications. In her "spare" time, she enjoys performing in community musical theater productions.

Irene and her husband, Tom—whom she describes as "my own romantic hero"—make their home in St. Louis, Missouri.

Never Say Goodbye
Irene Hannon

Love Inspired®

Published by Steeple Hill Books™

STEEPLE HILL BOOKS

Steeple
Hill™

ISBN 0-373-87182-1

NEVER SAY GOODBYE

Copyright © 2002 by Irene Hannon Gottlieb

Visit us at www.steeplehill.com

Printed in U.S.A.

Hope deferred makes the heart sick,
but a wish fulfilled is a tree of life.
—*Proverbs* 13:12

To my mom and dad, who fill my life with love
and add joy and grace to my days.

Chapter One

Three years.

Three long, lonely years.

Three years without freedom.

Three years without the woman he loved.

Three years of hell.

And now they were over.

Scott Mitchell turned and took one last look at the bleak gray walls of the high-security prison where he'd spent the past three years of his life.

Where he'd reached such depths of despair that he'd seriously considered suicide. Where he'd spent agonizing hours reliving the tragic accident that had taken the lives of two innocent people.

Where he'd lain awake night after night yearning for the tender touch and sheltering arms of the woman he loved...tormented by the knowledge that she never wanted to see him again.

Where he'd finally found something to cling to in a long-neglected interest in horticulture, a hobby that became a passion and offered a temporary escape from the drab walls to a world of color and beauty and new life.

Where he'd acknowledged his mistakes and straightened out his priorities.

And most important, where he'd slowly, one tentative step at a time, rebuilt his faith and reconnected with his God.

Scott drew a deep, cleansing breath as he stared at the hellish place that, ironically enough, had put him back on the road to heaven. But it had been a harsh, brutal journey. The abrupt transition from power lunches to prisoner, from a world where individual rights reigned supreme to a world where no rights existed had been harrowing. He'd been stripped of his dignity, reduced to a number, looked upon with contempt. He'd lost everything he ever cared about—and that didn't mean the designer suits or sports cars or country-club membership he'd once valued so highly. No, the loss was much more basic than that—the people he loved and his freedom. Dear God, how he'd missed those two things, which he'd always taken so much for granted!

But never again, he vowed. He was a different man now, with solid priorities and two very clear goals.

First, he intended to make his faith the guiding force in his life.

Second, he intended to win back the heart of the only woman he'd ever loved.

The first would be easy.

The second would take a miracle.

But Scott believed in miracles. He couldn't have survived these past three years without one.

Yet winning back Jess's love would take a miracle greater even than survival. He knew that. But with the Lord's guidance and grace, he believed it was possible. It had to be. Because on a spiritual level, he needed her forgiveness and love to complete his redemption. And on a very basic human level, he simply needed her.

And so he closed his eyes for a moment and prayed silently. *Dear Lord, show me the way to prove that I've changed, that my remorse is real and that I'm worthy of her love. Please give me the courage to persevere and steady me when I stumble. Don't let me lose heart if success is elusive. Help me remember that You are with me always, even on my darkest days, and that with You by my side, anything is possible.*

And then, with one last look at the forbidding walls, he stepped out of prison and into a new life.

Today was the day.

The man who had killed her daughter was free.

Jess Mitchell drew a long, unsteady breath and involuntarily tightened her grip on the coffee mug. Scott…her husband…the man she had once loved with all her heart…was free. And she hated him, with every fiber of her being. He'd destroyed their marriage and robbed her of the child of her heart, cutting short a life that had barely begun—as well as the life of a respected judge who'd died behind the wheel of the other car. That, too, had been a tragic loss, for he had been a man of principle and honor, a crusader for justice who had earned a reputation for integrity and courage.

As far as Jess was concerned, Scott deserved to rot in prison for the rest of his life.

Her hands suddenly began to shake and she carefully set the mug down, the taste of bitterness sharp on her tongue as she struggled to control a surge of anger—the same anger that had been her constant companion in the months following Elizabeth's death. Gradually a dull numbness had taken its place, insulating her from pain and allowing her to better cope with the world around her. But now the anger was back, and with it the raw pain.

Reaching out an unsteady hand toward the small glass-topped table in her breakfast nook, Jess shakily lowered herself into a chair. The February day was cold but bright, and a shaft of early-morning sun beamed through the skylight, illuminating the single daffodil in the bud vase in front of her. Gently she reached over and touched the delicate petals, so lovely but so fragile. There was something inspiring about daffodils, she thought with a bittersweet pang. The first harbingers of spring, they bloomed gloriously despite the risk of frost, announcing to those grown weary of the long, dark days of winter that the world would soon be warm and bright again. Perhaps that was why she had chosen this blossom for her table, she reflected. To give her courage to get through this difficult day.

Jess forced herself to take a deep, calming breath, thankful that at least she could once again find pleasure in the beauty of nature. She'd always loved flowers, and she was grateful that her work as public relations manager at the botanical garden gave her a ready supply. But today, even the exquisite beauty of this favorite flower couldn't dispel her gloom or the inexplicable sense of apprehension that filled her with a restless anxiety.

Jess forced herself to think through her emotions logically, a technique she'd picked up through six months of counseling following the accident. First of all, it was only natural for her feelings of anger and bitterness to bubble to the surface on the day her husband was being released from prison, she reasoned. Knowing that he was now a free man, once more a part of the real world—*her* world—made it impossible *not* to think about the trauma and the tragedy he had caused. It was a normal reaction.

But there was no reason to feel apprehensive, she reassured herself. Though they'd had no direct contact since Elizabeth's funeral, she'd made her feelings very clear to Scott shortly thereafter via a letter from her attorney. As far as she was concerned, no matter the outcome of the legal trial, he was a murderer. And she never wanted to see him again. Period. Those two points had been clearly communicated.

Nevertheless, Scott had written to her. Countless times. She'd returned every letter unopened and unanswered, so he had to know that the strength of her feelings hadn't diminished. She fervently hoped that he would honor her wishes and stay away.

For a moment Jess considered praying for that outcome, but she quickly dismissed the idea. She'd given up talking to the Lord a long time ago. Why bother?

He didn't listen anyway. In her darkest days her once-solid faith had offered no explanations, no solace for the senseless tragedy that had taken the life of her daughter and turned her world upside down. She was just as bitter toward God as she was toward her husband. Jess had always known that bad things sometimes happened to good people. Had somehow been able to reconcile that with her faith—until it happened to her. Then all the words of comfort she'd once offered to those caught in tragic situations seemed hollow and trite. All she knew was that the loving God she'd always believed in had let her down. Just as her husband had.

Jess pulled herself tiredly to her feet and drained her coffee cup, hoping the caffeine would energize her. She'd slept little last night—but what else was new? Her sleep pattern had been erratic for years. Sometimes, when she was very tired and if she stayed up late enough, she made it through a whole night. Other times she was plagued with nightmares. But worst of all were the times she'd awaken in the middle of the night, overcome with memories of the love she and Scott had shared early in their marriage, when their faith and their devotion to each other were the foundation of their life. On those nights, the loneliness and sense of loss would overwhelm her, filling her with such a hopeless yearning to recapture those early days of intimacy and unity that she'd suddenly discover tears running down her cheeks. And then she'd get up and prowl through the condo, looking for anything to distract her until the first light of day banished the memories of the night to the far corners of her mind.

Jess rinsed her cup, glanced at the bagel she'd planned to eat, and turned away, her stomach churning. Food rarely held much appeal anymore, especially today. Another sign of lingering depression. She knew that from counseling. She also knew there was a reason for her mood this morning. A trigger event. But she'd be okay. She'd get through today, and then she'd go on with the gradual process of rebuilding her life. And in time it would get easier. In time she would even feel normal again. Everyone told her that.

Jess clung to that hope. She had to. Because it was the only thing that helped her get through the endless stream of empty days—and the lonely, memory-filled nights.

"Jess?"

It was one word. Only one word, spoken through a poor connection. But she knew that voice as well as her own. You couldn't live with a man for eight years without learning the nuances of his every inflection.

Jess's heart stopped, then slammed into triple time. Her lungs seemed paralyzed, and she struggled to take a breath, fighting a wave of light-headedness. In the two days since Scott's release, she'd gradually calmed down, convinced herself that he was going to leave her alone.

But she'd been wrong.

Her first impulse was to simply hang up. But if he was still as single-minded and determined as he'd once been, he'd just call again, she realized in panic. Should she talk to him, reiterate that she wanted nothing to do with him? Or should she simply call her lawyer and let him handle the situation?

"Jess? Are you there?"

Softer now, sounding as unsteady as she felt, his voice still had that intimate, husky cadence that had always set her pulse racing. And she didn't want to hear it. Not now. Not ever. Without uttering a word—*unable* to utter a word—she simply followed her instinct. She hung up.

Scott heard the soft but very definitive click and slowly let out his breath. It had taken him an hour to work up the courage to call Jess—once he'd found her number. He knew she'd sold the house, because during the past year his letters had been returned marked "no forwarding address." But he was reasonably certain she'd still be in St. Louis. She'd always been close to her parents, and he was sure she'd relied on them heavily during the traumatic months following the accident and trial. So he'd let his fingers do the walking, and on the third try he had connected with her. But the connection had been purely electronic, he acknowledged with a sigh. And broken very quickly.

Slowly Scott replaced the receiver of the pay phone, then leaned back against the concrete wall of the filling station and allowed his gaze to rise above the rundown buildings around him. His breath billowed in frosty clouds toward the cobalt-blue sky, but even in his inadequate jacket he didn't feel the cold. His heart was pounding so hard, the blood rushing so quickly through his veins, that he was actually too warm.

Scott had hoped to accomplish several things with

his phone call. Test the waters, for one. And Jess's silent hang-up had given him a definite reading on that: very cold. He'd also wanted to verify her address. That goal, too, had been accomplished. Though she hadn't said a word, he knew with absolute certainty that he'd reached the right number. He could sense her presence, her energy, coming through the line.

But more than anything, he'd simply wanted to hear the expressive, slightly husky voice that had filled his dreams for three long years. He'd clung to the memory of her bell-like laughter and the sometimes teasing, sometimes tender, sometimes curious and *always* enthusiastic tone that so clearly reflected her dynamic personality. Today he'd hoped to turn memory into reality. Even one word would have been enough to sustain him temporarily. On that score, however, he'd been less successful.

But he would try again.

And next time it would be in person.

"You seem quiet today, Jess. Everything okay?"

Jess looked at her father, then transferred her gaze to her mother. Though the question had been asked calmly and conversationally, she felt their undertone of worry. They'd seen her through some rough times over the past few years, had stood by her through her deepest despair, almost forcibly taking her to counseling sessions when all she'd wanted to do was huddle in bed under the covers in a dark room. As a result, they had come to learn every nuance of her moods.

While she was deeply grateful for their steadfast caring, it was a bit disconcerting to know that there was little she could hide from them. Certainly nothing as traumatic as Scott's phone call. She realized now that she should have told them about Scott's upcoming release two weeks ago, when her attorney had called to alert her. But she had hoped there would be no need to worry them. Had hoped Scott would stay away and not disrupt the delicate balance of her fragile existence. But that hope had been in vain, and now she was faced with the difficult task of telling her parents about Scott's release—and his call.

Carefully Jess set her fork down and reached for her glass of water, willing her hand not to shake as she took a sip. "I'm fine," she replied, struggling with limited success to keep her voice steady, "but I was a little upset yesterday. S-Scott called."

Her mother's fork clattered to her plate, and her eyes grew wide. Her father looked equally shaken, though his shock quickly gave way to anger as his face grew hard and his mouth settled into a thin, unforgiving line.

"What do you mean, Scott called?" he said, his voice taut with tension.

Jess drew a shaky breath and met his disturbed gaze. "He's out, Dad. John Kane called a few days ago to tell me that he was being released early for good behavior."

Jess couldn't quite make out her father's muttered comment, but she knew from his tone that it wasn't pretty. He threw his napkin onto the table and rose to pace agitatedly.

"Good behavior? From a murderer? That's ridiculous. He deserved every second of his five-year sentence—if not more.''

"Frank, please try not to get upset," Jess's mother pleaded, her own face pinched and drawn. "You know this isn't good for your blood pressure."

He paused and glared at his wife. "How can you be so calm about this, Clare? This is the man who killed your granddaughter and almost ruined your daughter's life."

Clare's eyes filled with tears and she groped in the pocket of her skirt for a tissue. "I know, Frank. I'm not happy about it, either. But what can we do?"

He began to pace again, and Jess could feel his seething frustration. "We can stop him from calling Jess, for one thing. If he's bothering her, that's harassment. We can get a restraining order."

"Please Dad…Mom…it's okay. That's not necessary," Jess assured them with more calm than she felt. "He only called once. And I didn't even talk to him. I just hung up."

That seemed to placate Frank, and after a moment he took his seat again. "Well, that's good. You did the right thing, sweetie. He ought to get the message. And if he doesn't, I'll call John and he'll take care of it. Okay?"

"Okay, Dad."

Clare reached over and took Jess's hand, twin lines of worry furrowing her brow. "Are you sure, honey? Because if you're scared, we can call John right now."

Jess stared at her mother. Scared? Of Scott? That thought had never even entered her mind. In fact, it was almost ludicrous. She might hate her husband for what he had done to her daughter and for ruining her life, but he wasn't a violent man.

"Why would I be scared, Mom?"

Clare's frown deepened. "Well, it's been three years, Jess," she said carefully. "And prison is a hard place, from what I've read. It can...do things to a person. Change them. Did he sound angry, or threatening?"

Jess thought back to the few words Scott had spoken on the phone. There had been absolutely no hint of anger or threat in his voice. On the contrary. He'd sounded anxious. And shaky. And...hungry.

Now it was Jess's turn to frown. *Hungry.* What an odd word to pop into her mind. And yet it was accurate, she realized. There had been a raw need in his voice when he'd spoken her name. As if he *had* to hear her voice, to connect with her in some tangible way. It was an oddly disconcerting realization.

"Jess?"

Her mother's anxious voice brought her back to the present, and she summoned up a reassuring smile. "No, Mom. He didn't sound angry. He sounded...the same."

"I can't believe he called you," Frank said, a thread of anger still running through his voice. "Why would he do that, when you made it clear you never wanted to see him again?"

"I don't know, Dad." Her own voice was suddenly weary.

"Well, let's forget about it as best we can and enjoy our dinner," Clare suggested, forcibly lightening her tone as she sent a "let-it-drop-for-now" look to her husband. "Your dad's right, honey. Hanging up on him was the best thing you could have done. He's a smart man. He'll get the message. You'll probably never hear from him again. Now, how about another biscuit?"

As Jess took the proffered breadbasket, she hoped her mother was right about Scott. But she wasn't optimistic. She'd heard his voice. And she didn't think he was going to give up until she talked with him. Which was something she did *not* want to do.

Maybe a restraining order was in her future after all.

A gust of frigid air whipped past, and Scott turned up the collar of his denim jacket before jamming his hands into the pockets of his jeans. He was chilled to the bone after waiting at the bus stop for thirty minutes, and the inadequate heater on the public conveyance had done little to dispel the numbing cold. The greenhouse looming in front of him promised a haven from the freezing temperatures, and he quickened his pace, breathing a sigh of relief as he stepped into the balmy oasis.

For a moment Scott just stood there, letting the welcome warmth seep through his pores as he scanned the interior. The facility was well maintained, with half of the space devoted to row after row of tagged trays containing tiny seedlings, while larger pots of healthy-looking perennials occupied the other half. Large rubber hoses lay neatly coiled at periodic intervals, and hanging pots were spaced methodically above the seedlings. The operation appeared to be orderly and well run, Scott noted with approval.

"You must be Scott."

At the sound of the gravelly voice, Scott turned. An older man had entered the greenhouse by a side door and now stood observing him from several yards away. Make that "assessing him," Scott thought wryly, as the man's shrewd, slightly narrowed eyes studied him. Scott took the opportunity to look him over, as well. An unlit cigar was clamped between his teeth, and his fists were planted on his hips. His white hair was closely cropped in a no-nonsense style, and his attire—worn jeans that molded comfortably to his lean frame, and an open fleece-lined jacket that revealed a T-shirt containing the words Lawson Landscaping—spoke more to practicality than style. His stance and tone were definitely intimidating enough to scare off most potential job applicants.

But Scott wanted this job. Reverend Young, one of the local clergy who volunteered as a prison chaplain, had warned him when he set up the interview that Seth Lawson was a fair but hard taskmaster. That he expected a lot and cut no slack. But that was okay with Scott. He wasn't looking for any favors. He just wanted a chance to start over. And as an ex-con himself who had served time for armed robbery many years before, Seth was sometimes willing to give newly released prisoners that chance. Which was more than could be said for a lot of employers. Or people in general. Even though ex-cons had served their time and paid their debt, society was often unwilling to take them back. So the odds were stacked against them.

But Scott didn't intend to become another statistic. With the help of people like Reverend Young and Seth Lawson, he would make it. He straightened his shoulders and gazed steadily into the older man's razor-sharp, intensely blue eyes. "That's right. I'm Scott Mitchell."

Seth studied Scott for another moment, then nodded toward the rear of the greenhouse. "Office is back there. Let's talk."

He led the way to a compact but well-equipped office furnished with three unoccupied desks, several filing cabinets, a fax machine and a copier. Instead of sitting behind one of the desks, however, he continued toward a small conference room at the back, pausing as he passed the coffeemaker.

"Want a cup?"

Scott nodded, trying not to appear too eager. He was still trying to shake the February chill, and coffee would help. "Thanks."

"Cream?"

"Black."

Seth poured two cups, then moved into the conference room, shrugged out of his jacket and sat down at the round table. Scott followed suit—but he left his coat on.

"So tell me why you want this job," Seth said without preamble, chewing on his cigar.

Scott wrapped his hands around the coffee cup, letting the warmth seep into his numb fingers. "I need a job," he said honestly. "More than that, I need a chance to start over. I know something about horticulture, and I don't want a job with walls. This sounded perfect.''

"It's far from perfect," Seth replied bluntly. "Most guys don't last more than a few weeks. It's hard work. Dirty work. And the pay's not great.''

"I'm not afraid of hard work. Or dirt. And I don't need much money.''

Seth considered that answer for a moment. "You have any family?''

A spasm of pain ricocheted through Scott's eyes. "I have a sister and brother-in-law in Chicago. And three nephews.''

Seth glanced pointedly at the wedding ring on Scott's left hand. "That it?''

Scott drew an unsteady breath. "I also have a wife. In name, at least. She doesn't believe in divorce. But she never wants to see me again.''

"Too bad. It helps to have family and friends around when you get out. But a lot of people can't handle the stigma of being associated with an ex-con.''

"Jess isn't like that.''

Seth's eyebrows rose. "But she never wants to see you again.''

Scott swallowed past the lump in his throat. "For good reason. I made some bad mistakes.''

"You also paid for them.''

"In the eyes of society, maybe. I'm not sure about in the eyes of God.''

Seth considered that for a moment. "How long were you in?''

"Three years.''

"What did you do before?''

"I was in marketing."

When he named the company, Seth's eyebrows rose. "Were you in for one of those white-collar crimes?"

Scott frowned. "Didn't Reverend Young tell you?"

Seth shrugged. "Didn't ask. Doesn't matter. I judge people by who they are now, not what they did years ago. I was just curious. Don't get too many guys in here with your polish."

Scott took a sip of the scalding liquid, which suddenly tasted bitter on his tongue. "I'm surprised there's any polish left," he said quietly.

Seth looked at him shrewdly. "It's rough in there, all right. Takes a lot out of a man."

"Yeah."

"You have any money?"

Scott frowned again. The conversation was all over the place and he was having a hard time keeping up. "No."

"You're still married. Anything still in your name?"

"No. I signed it all over to Jess when I was convicted."

"Think she might give you a loan to get you started?"

"I don't plan to ask."

Seth folded his arms across his chest. "Be pretty hard to live on the salary I'm offering."

"I'll manage. I don't need much. Just a chance."

Seth nodded shortly. "That I can give you." He reached into his pocket, withdrew a wallet and laid several fifty-dollar bills on the table. "Consider this an advance on your salary. Get yourself a warm coat and some sturdy shoes. Be here tomorrow at seven.''

Scott looked at the money. There was a time when he would drop twice that amount on a business dinner with several colleagues. In those days, money had meant prestige and power. Now it just meant survival. Funny how dramatically things had changed, he reflected. Slowly he reached for the bills and carefully folded them over. ''Thank you,'' he said. ''For the loan. And for taking me on.''

Seth shrugged and stood up. ''Don't thank me yet. It's hard, dirty work. You might not last a week.''

''I'll last.'' The statement was made quietly—but with absolute conviction.

Seth looked at him speculatively, but made no comment. Instead he turned and led the way to the door. ''Tomorrow morning. Seven sharp.''

''I'll be here.'' Scott extended his hand, and Seth took it in a firm grip. The older man's probing gaze seemed to go right to Scott's heart.

''I was in your shoes once,'' he said evenly. ''I know how hard it is to lose everything. And society doesn't make it easy to start over. Some guys make it. Some don't. The bitter ones never do. Neither do the ones who can't admit their mistakes. I figure you're gonna make it.''

Scott felt a prickling behind his eyelids. For some reason this stranger's words of encouragement touched him deeply. ''I figure I am, too.''

''Reverend Young tells me you're a churchgoing man. That gives you a leg up right there.''

''It also gives me hope.''

"Hope is a good thing to have."

"It's the *only* thing I have right now."

"Maybe that's enough. For right now," Seth said sagely. "One thing you learn in this business. Patience. Things happen in their own time." He nodded toward a pot where new green leaves were just beginning to push their way through the dirt. "You take care of plants, give them light and warmth and water, and in time they'll flower. You can help the process along, but you can't make them bloom until they're ready. Same with a lot of things in life. Especially people."

Scott thought of Jess, and the slow, daunting task of trying to win back her love. "Yeah," he said heavily.

"But remember one thing. Spring always comes."

Scott looked at Seth, taken aback by the man's philosophical—and poetic—insight. No wonder Reverend Young had spoken so highly of him. "I like that thought."

Seth shrugged, the philosophical moment clearly over. "Good. Now go buy that coat. You'll need it tomorrow," he said briskly. A movement on the far side of the greenhouse suddenly caught his attention, and he turned. "Jason? Wait up!" he called. He looked back at Scott. "Gotta talk to him about the spring shipment of dogwood trees. See you tomorrow."

Scott watched the older man stride down the length of the greenhouse, impressed and encouraged by their encounter. This job was going to work out fine. He could sense it.

He turned up his collar and moved toward the door, bracing himself for the blast of cold air waiting for him on the other side. Seth was right, he thought wryly. The first order of business was a warm coat.

He was right about something else, too, Scott acknowledged as he stepped into the frigid February air and began the long, chilling trek to the bus stop.

No matter how cold, how inhospitable, how merciless the winter is, spring always comes.

It was a good thought, Scott reflected. An uplifting thought. And he resolved to hold on to it—no matter what lay ahead in the weeks to come.

Chapter Two

"Scott? Is everything all right?"

Scott smiled as his sister's voice came over the line. "Everything's fine. It just took me a couple of days to get settled."

"I can't believe Joe got appendicitis the day before you got out! We wanted to pick you up and help you get settled," she fretted. "Do you have a place to stay? Are you eating?"

His smile deepened. Karen had always been a mother hen, even more so since their own mother had died five years before. And her mothering instincts had intensified since he'd been in prison—for which he was deeply grateful. Other than Reverend Young, she'd been his lifeline, his only contact with the outside world for three long years. He would never forget her steadfast support and her willingness to stand by him despite the tragic mistakes he'd made—nor her long monthly trek to visit him. "Yes to both. How's Joe?"

"He'll live. It's you I've been worrying about. Why didn't you call sooner?"

"I did call. Almost as soon as I walked out the gates."

"But that was three days ago!"

"I've been busy ever since. I had to look at the apartments Reverend Young lined up, and I had an interview at the nursery today."

"Did you get the job?"

"Yes. It was the strangest interview I've ever had, but I have a feeling things will work out fine."

"Good. I know you were counting on that job." There was a slight pause, and when she spoke again he could hear the frown in her voice. "Listen, where are you?"

"In my apartment."

"So you have a phone. Give me the number." Scott complied, then Karen read it back to confirm. "Okay. I'm hanging up and calling you right back," she said briskly. "You can't afford this call."

"Karen, I'm fine. You don't have to—"

"I'm hanging up. Bye."

The line went dead and Scott shook his head, smiling with equal parts affection and exasperation. As a stay-at-home mom with three boys, Karen wasn't exactly rolling in dough, either. But when she got a notion in her head, there was no stopping her.

A moment later the phone rang and Scott reached for it. "That wasn't necessary, you know."

"Listen, big brother, do me a favor, okay? Let people help you if they want to. I just wish you'd come up here for a few weeks, like I asked you to."

"I appreciate the offer, Karen. I really do. But I need to get back into the real world sooner or later. It might as well be sooner."

He could hear her sigh of frustration over the wire. "Look, Scott, you could use a break. You deserve it. I was there, remember? I saw you the first Friday of every month. You lost forty pounds in six months. You looked like death. I worried about you night and day. You never talked about life in there, but I know it was hell. I know how close you came to…giving up." She took a deep breath, and when she resumed speaking, there was a tremor in her voice. "Dear God, my heart bled for you every time I walked out the door and had to leave you behind. Do you know where I went when I left, after my first five or six visits? To the ladies' room to throw up. I just couldn't bear that you were in that place, and that I couldn't do anything to help you."

Her voice broke, and Scott felt as if someone had kicked him in the gut. Karen had never before even *hinted* at the emotional toll her visits had taken. Just the opposite. She'd always been upbeat and chatty, working hard to cheer him up by telling him humorous anecdotes about the family, passing on drawings the boys had done for him, sharing photos of the birthday parties and Christmases he'd missed. Those visits had been the only thing that kept him going in those early months. Because of her he had still felt connected to the outside world. Because of her he was able for a brief time to feel human again. But if he'd known the emotional toll it had taken on her, he would never have let her come. "I'm so sorry, Karen," he said, his voice anguished. "I had no idea."

"That was the intent." Her voice still sounded a bit shaky, but she quickly got it under control. "I know you, big brother. If you'd had any idea what those visits did to me, you'd have told me to stop coming. And I *wanted* to be there for you. But it's over now. I only brought it up because I want you to know that I realize how horrible it was. And I think you need to take some time to readjust. To rest. To decompress. That's why I wanted you to come up to Chicago and stay with us for a while. I still wish you would."

Scott felt overwhelmed by a rush of love and gratitude, and his throat tightened with emotion. Karen's love and support were blessings for which he would always be grateful. "I love you for offering, sis," he said, his own voice none too steady. "You don't know how much it means to me. Just like your visits. In case I haven't told you—and I probably haven't, because men aren't always too good at that communication thing—I want you to know that I wouldn't have made it without them. Knowing you were coming back, that I wasn't totally alone, that someone cared and was thinking about me, is the only thing that got me through those early months. You were my rock."

He heard Karen sniff over the wire. "Who says men aren't good at communication? You just got an A," she said tearily. She paused to blow her nose, and when she continued her voice was steadier. "Okay, now, enough of this mushy stuff. If you won't come up, then let me send you a little money to tide you over."

"I'm fine, sis."

"You can pay it back, okay? Consider it a loan."

"I have a job. And a place to live. I'm fine. Really."

Another exasperated sigh. "You are one stubborn man, you know that?"

He grinned. "I think it runs in the family."

"Very funny. Okay, have it your way. What's your address?"

He hesitated. "No money. Promise."

She muttered something he couldn't make out. "Fine. No money."

He gave her the information, and then glanced at his watch. "This call is costing you a fortune."

"Look, forget the money for a minute, okay? Indulge me. We've got three years of catching up to do *without* a guard standing over our shoulder. Which reminds me…do you think you'll be ready for a visitor soon?"

"You don't have to make a special trip down, Karen."

"Hey, just because you're out of prison doesn't mean you're going to shake me that easily. I'm heading down to check on you as soon as Joe's mother comes to visit in mid-March. She can help him with the kids while I'm gone. I'll consider it a vacation. Trust me—I deserve it. We've been decimated by the flu this winter, and guess who's been playing nurse?"

Scott chuckled. "When you put it that way, how can I refuse?"

"You can't," she replied pertly.

He glanced around the tiny furnished apartment,

with its threadbare upholstery, worn carpeting and nicked furniture. He could just imagine what Karen would say about his living conditions. "Just don't expect the Ritz, okay?" he cautioned.

She gave an unladylike snort. "With three kids and twenty more years to go on the mortgage, the Ritz is out of my league, anyway."

But not this far out, Scott thought as his gaze once more traveled around the shabby apartment. She would *not* be happy to find him living in these conditions. But that was a battle for another day. "Tell Joe and the kids I said hi."

"Will do." There was a slight hesitation, and when Karen spoke again her voice was cautious. "Listen, I don't mean to be nosy, but…have you talked to Jess?"

Scott's smile faded. "Yes."

"Any luck?"

"She hung up on me."

Karen sighed. "I'm sorry, Scott."

"It's okay. I didn't expect her to welcome me with open arms."

"Hang in there, okay?"

"I will. Believe me, I'm an expert at that after the past three years. I've learned to take everything a day at a time."

"Not a bad philosophy. Listen, I'll call again in a couple of days. Promise to take care of yourself in the meantime?"

"Count on it."

"You'll let me know if you need anything?"

"Absolutely."

"Okay. I'll let you go for now. And Scott... welcome back."

As they said their goodbyes and Scott replaced the receiver, he thought about Karen's parting words. *Welcome back.* They had a nice sound. And it felt wonderful to be back. To be free.

But the words he really wanted to hear were *Welcome home.* And those could come from only one person.

Jess slammed the car door shut with her hip, juggling a briefcase, a bag of groceries and a shoulder purse. She didn't usually work on Saturdays, but with the opening of the orchid show only a few days away she'd needed to tie up a few loose ends on publicity. The weather was too nice for indoor pursuits, though, she thought as she made her way toward her condo. The early-March day was unseasonably warm. Almost balmy, in fact. It was like a sneak preview of spring—and perfect for a nice long walk, she decided. As soon as she put away the groceries, she would change into her walking shoes and...

"Hello, Jess."

Startled, Jess came to an abrupt stop as the man who had once been the center of her world stepped out of the shadows of a spruce tree. The bag of groceries slipped from her grasp, and only Scott's quick reflexes kept it from hitting the sidewalk. He moved swiftly toward her and made a successful grab for it, which salvaged the canned goods—but dented her heart. Only inches away, his tangible, physical presence drove the breath from her lungs and she stumbled

backward, desperately trying to put distance between
them, unable to deal with the sudden, too-close proximity. She stared at him, wide-eyed, her hand moving
involuntarily to her throat, frozen to the spot as she
tried to process the impressions bombarding her
senses.

There was no question that the man who stood motionless six feet in front of her, balancing the rescued
grocery bag easily in one arm, was Scott. Absolutely
no question. She would recognize him anywhere. Yet
he was different. And it was more than the physical
changes, though they were quite apparent, as well. For
one thing, his dark hair now contained a sprinkling of
silver at the temples. There were more lines on his
face, which oddly enough seemed to suggest character
rather than age. And he looked more toned than she'd
ever seen him. His jeans fit his lean form like a second
skin, and his T-shirt hugged a broad, muscular chest
and revealed well-developed biceps. Scott had always
been a handsome man. Now his virility was almost
tangible.

But the physical changes weren't what gave Jess
pause. It was something else, something almost inde-
finable. A sense of quiet calm, of acceptance, of surrender almost. As if he'd somehow found a way to
deal with all of the tragedy and pain and horror, made
his peace with it and moved on. In the depths of his
brown eyes she saw serenity, and a wave of envy
surged over her. How had he been able to achieve that
when it had so utterly eluded her? she wondered re-
sentfully. Nothing seemed left of his restless, driving
ambition, which had grown stronger and stronger until

it had become the center of his life and had driven a wedge into their marriage. In its place was a quiet, appealing gentleness.

But there were other things in his eyes as well, she realized. Things that were even closer to the surface and equally disturbing in a very different way. Hunger. Need. And undisguised love. All of which left her completely off balance and confused.

While Jess struggled to come to grips with her volatile emotions, Scott took stock of the woman who had added so much joy to his life and filled his dreams for the past three years. She, too, was different than he remembered, and the changes troubled him. There was an unfamiliar tautness to her face, as if the skin was stretched too tightly over the fine bone structure beneath. And she seemed tense, tightly coiled, radiating an unsettling nervous energy that suggested she might snap at the least provocation.

Scott had known his unexpected appearance would upset her. But he sensed that Jess's tension went far deeper and was of a much longer-term nature. As if it was the norm rather than a momentary reaction. She seemed somehow…brittle, as if she would break at the slightest touch. And far too thin, he concluded with a sweeping gaze. The fluid silk blouse that hugged her upper body suggested angular lines and sharp edges rather than the soft curves he remembered, and the circumference of the belt of her black slacks seemed tiny. Jess had always been slender, but now she was just plain skinny. His gaze moved back to her deep green eyes, and there he noticed the greatest change of all. Gone was the sparkle of joy with which she had always greeted each new day. In its place was a deep-seated sadness that was clearly of long duration.

Scott's gut twisted painfully. He was well aware of the pain he'd caused Jess. Had always recognized it on an intellectual level. But now, confronted with the physical evidence of it, he knew that the hell he'd been through in prison had been no worse than her own private hell, which had left her shattered and fragile and heartbreakingly vulnerable.

Scott wanted to go to her, to pull her into his arms and promise to take away her pain, to care for her, to never hurt her again. But he knew his words would fall on deaf ears. Because he was the *cause* of her pain. He *hadn't* been able to care for her in her greatest time of need. And there was no reason for her to believe that he would never hurt her again. Winning her back, he realized with a heavy heart, would be an even more daunting task than he'd imagined.

As he gazed at her, at the white-knuckled grip she had on her briefcase, at her face suddenly grown pale, he realized that she was trembling. Badly. She suddenly swayed ever so slightly, but when he instinctively took a step toward her she backed away in alarm, only to lose her balance as she tottered half on and half off the concrete walk. A moment later she lost her footing and found herself sprawled on the ground.

In a flash, Scott set the groceries on the walk and knelt beside her, his concerned eyes only inches from hers, his voice worried, his hand on her arm.

"I'm sorry, Jess. I didn't mean to startle you. Are you okay?"

She stared at him, hardly able to breathe. She looked at his hand—strong, gentle and achingly familiar—on her arm, and her heart stopped, then slammed into overdrive. Dear God, why was she being tormented this way? she cried silently. She'd never wanted to see this man again! She hated him! Hated how his ambition had eaten away at their marriage. Hated how he'd begun to turn to alcohol to relieve the tension of stress-filled days in the business world. Hated how he'd taken the deadly chance that fateful night that ruined her life and ended two others. And hated how, in his presence, she was confronted again by the "if only" that had hung like a dark cloud over her life ever since the tragic accident. The "if only" that said her daughter might not have died if she'd insisted on driving that night instead of letting Scott take the wheel.

Choking back a sob, she scrambled to her feet, filled with an urgent need to get away from Scott. For some reason she sensed danger. Not of a physical nature. But danger nonetheless. She had to get to the safety of her condo, where she could bolt the door against this intrusion on her life. Yet even as she slung her purse over her shoulder and reached for her briefcase, a sick feeling in the pit of her stomach told her that she couldn't bolt the door against this intrusion on her heart. That her life was once again about to be turned upside down. Blinded by tears, she groped for the grocery bag, but Scott beat her to it.

"Let me help." He reached for it and swung it up into his arm.

She hesitated for only a moment. Then, without a word, she turned and headed for her condo, half running as she dug through her purse for her keys, struggling to control the tears that threatened to spill from her eyes.

"Jess, please."

He was behind her. Following her. Harassing her. She walked more quickly.

"Please, Jess. I just want to talk to you."

Something in his tone made her step falter for a moment, but then, angry at herself for allowing the choked entreaty in his voice to affect her, she resolutely quickened her pace.

He didn't speak again, but she knew he was still behind her. Her hand was shaking so badly when she reached her door that she had difficulty fitting her key in the lock. Then, just when she thought she was home free, it slipped from her fingers and clattered to the concrete steps.

Before she could react, he reached down and retrieved it. Panic once more engulfed her. Now she was trapped. Tears of frustration spilled from her eyes, and she swiped at them angrily and desperately tried to figure out what to do. But her brain seemed to have shifted into neutral.

To her surprise, however, Scott didn't hold her hostage. After only a moment's hesitation he reached past her and fitted the key into the lock. It took him two tries, and she noted with surprise that his hands were almost as unsteady as hers. After he turned the key, he stepped back.

"I'll leave your groceries on the step," he said quietly.

She heard the rustle of the paper bag as he deposited

the sack, and she reached for the knob, prepared to flee, planning to retrieve the groceries later. But then he spoke again.

"I never had a chance to say this in person, Jess. And I know it doesn't change anything. But I want you to know how sorry I am…about everything. I made a lot of mistakes. Tragic mistakes that I regret with all my heart. But the one thing that wasn't a mistake was loving you."

The raw pain, the passion, in his voice jolted her, compelled her with a force she couldn't ignore to turn and face the man she had once loved. He was standing a couple of feet away, his hands jammed into the pockets of his jeans, his face filled with such sadness and remorse that she couldn't doubt the truth of his words. But being sorry didn't change a thing, she thought bitterly as the tears she'd tried so hard to contain suddenly spilled out of her eyes.

Scott watched helplessly, feeling physically sick. He'd been prepared to face Jess's anger. But he hadn't been prepared to watch her crumble in front of his eyes. He lifted a hand in an imploring gesture, then let it drop back to his side. "Dear God, Jess, I'm so sorry," he repeated hoarsely, his voice choked.

She shook her head and reached again for the doorknob. "It's too late," she whispered brokenly. Then she slipped inside, shutting the door firmly behind her. A moment later he heard the bolt slide into place.

For several minutes Scott simply stood there staring at the closed door, struck by the symbolism. She was shutting him out of her life…and her heart. Her three words said it all. *It's too late.*

But Scott didn't believe it was too late. *Couldn't* believe it. Because it was impossible to envision a future without Jess. He needed her...just as he believed she needed him. They had linked their destinies once, for better, for worse, and Jess had abided by their vows despite the tragedy that had befallen them. Though they were married in name only at the moment, he clung to the hope that with God's help, Jess would eventually come to realize that he was a changed man. That his remorse was real. That his love for her had not only endured but grown during their long years apart. And that the joyous, vibrant, life-giving love they had once shared could live again.

As he turned away, Scott knew that his prospects seemed bleak. But he wouldn't give up. Because he believed in the truth of Seth's philosophy.

Spring always comes.

"Scott. It's good to see you." Reverend Young grasped Scott's hand warmly. "I was hoping you'd make it to services."

"It was a little tricky," Scott admitted. "The buses run on an entirely different schedule on the weekends."

The minister frowned. "I must admit I forgot about your lack of transportation. We'll find you a ride from now on."

"I don't want to put anyone out, Reverend. The bus worked out fine."

The minister laid a kindly hand on his shoulder. "There are a lot of good, Christian people out there, Scott. Give them a chance to put their beliefs into action."

Scott smiled. "It's pretty hard to refuse when you put it that way."

"Sometimes accepting help is much harder than giving it," he acknowledged. "So are you settled in? Everything going okay?"

"So far so good."

"How are you and Seth getting on?"

Scott grinned. "Fine. I think. He's not much of a talker."

Reverend Young chuckled. "True enough. But he's a good man. Fair and honest and dependable. He's not much of a churchgoer, but he really lives the golden rule. Is the work okay? I know he expects a lot."

"He does. But I don't mind hard work. Which is a good thing, because he's got a lot of commercial land-scaping contracts and spring is a busy time. Let me put it this way...I rarely have any trouble sleeping." Except for the nights when even bone-weary fatigue couldn't overcome the longing in his heart for Jess, he added silently as a shadow swept across his eyes. Then he forced his thoughts in a different direction. "You have a nice church here, Reverend," he complimented the man, glancing around the grounds. "It's just like you described."

The minister nodded in satisfaction. "We've come a long way since this land was donated five years ago. Would you like to see the back?"

"Sure."

They made their way around the building, which stood on a slight rise that overlooked a small tree-ringed pond. Though it was in a suburban area, the grounds were quiet and secluded. "I come back here when I need a few moments to refresh my soul," the minister said. "It's a nice spot, isn't it?"

"Very. What's going on back there?" Scott nodded toward the edge of the pond, where some sort of construction project was in progress.

"One of our members thought a gazebo would be a nice addition, and offered to build one."

"I agree." Scott eyed the terrain critically. "Have you thought about adding a meditation garden, as well? It's a perfect spot for one."

The minister looked at him in surprise. "Frankly, no. Though I have to say the idea has appeal."

"I'd be happy to draw up some plans for you. And if the church could afford to invest in some plants and trees, I'd be glad to do the work."

Reverend Young smiled. "You work all week, Scott," he reminded the younger man gently. "Everyone needs a day of rest."

Scott shrugged. "It would give me a lot of pleasure to create a place of beauty that people could enjoy. I wouldn't consider it work. And I have the time."

The minister studied him for a moment. "You need to take some time for yourself, Scott. And for Jess."

Scott stared out over the placid waters of the lake. Reverend Young knew his most intimate secrets and dreams, more so even than Karen. He'd tried to shield her as much as possible from his private demons, though clearly she'd picked up on far more than he'd realized. But with Reverend Young it had been different. The minister had been there when Scott was at his lowest ebb, when he'd given up on life, when he'd been able to see only darkness on the horizon. And he'd made the long journey to prison numerous times in those days just to see Scott, to walk with him through the valley of darkness, until light had finally begun to dawn on the dark horizon. If Karen had saved

Scott by giving him abiding love, Reverend Young had saved him by giving him abiding faith.

"Things aren't going well with Jess," Scott said quietly.

"Have you talked to her?"

"Yes. The first time she hung up on me without saying a word. The second time I waited for her at her condo. But she couldn't get away from me fast enough. She just said it was too late and closed the door in my face."

"You knew it wouldn't be easy."

Scott sighed. "Yeah."

"Hate is a difficult thing to overcome, Scott. And forgiveness doesn't come easily for many people."

Scott frowned. "That's the odd thing, Reverend. I expected hate. And anger. But what I saw in Jess was more…I don't know. Confusion. Fear. Pain. It was almost as if the whole thing happened four days ago, not almost four years ago."

"I'm sure your release brought back all the memories. Made them seem fresh again. She may need some time to sort through her feelings now that you're back in her life. To deal with unresolved issues."

"So should I back off? Wait awhile?"

"You might want to move slowly," the minister counseled. "Even though I know that's hard to do. But I know the Lord will show you the way if you put your trust in Him."

Scott sighed and shook his head. "Patience is one of those virtues I'm still working on, Reverend."

The minister smiled sympathetically. "You and millions of other people." Then he turned back toward the lake, a thoughtful expression on his face. "You know, I think a garden would be just the thing for the gazebo. I'll run it by the church council at our meeting this week and let you know. Besides, gardening is a good way to develop patience," he added, his eyes twinkling as the two men headed back to the front of the church.

Scott grinned. "You sound like Seth."

The minister chuckled. "He's quite a philosopher, isn't he?" As they prepared to part, the minister laid a hand on Scott's shoulder, his eyes once more serious. "Hang in there, okay? I'll keep you in my prayers."

Scott took the minister's hand in a firm clasp. "Thanks. I can use them."

The minister smiled. "That's my job. You plant trees. I plant prayers. But both send out roots. We just need to do our part."

Scott thought about the aptness of Reverend Young's analogy as he headed back to his apartment. The visible signs of his relationship with Jess, the arching branches and beautiful blooms, had been ruthlessly chopped off at ground level. To the eye it had died. But Scott believed with all his heart that the roots were still there, filled with life. That with nurturing, tender new shoots would spring from the parched ground.

It was up to him to make that happen. And with the Lord's help and guidance, he would find a way.

Chapter Three

Jess glanced at her bedside clock and groaned. Three in the morning—only ten minutes later than when she'd last checked. Since going to bed four hours earlier, she'd logged all of thirty minutes' sleep, she calculated wearily. This was going to be one of those nights. Meaning tomorrow would be a very long day at work.

With a resigned sigh she threw back the covers, swung her feet to the floor and reached for her robe. Maybe a soothing cup of herbal tea would help, she thought hopefully as she padded toward the kitchen. Mechanically she filled the kettle, turned on the stove, dropped a tea bag into a mug. But her mind was elsewhere. Namely, on her encounter with Scott the day before.

She'd slept little last night and had spent most of today trying, with some success, to avoid thinking about Scott. But she had far less control over her *sub-*

conscious thoughts, and they kept bubbling to the surface each time she began to drift to sleep.

The whistle of the kettle distracted her momentarily, and she automatically went through the motions of making her tea. Then she carried it to the living room and sank into a comfortable chair, letting her gaze rest on the photograph of Elizabeth prominently displayed on the coffee table. Her daughter's smile was infectious, her four-year-old eyes bright with enthusiasm and lively intelligence and the sheer joy of life so common in the very young. She would be almost eight now. Finishing up second grade. Looking far more grown-up than she had in this photo.

If.

Jess drew an unsteady breath. She knew it didn't do any good to keep rehashing the past. To keep asking the "what if?" questions. Her therapist had stressed that over and over again. You had to deal with the bad things in your life, then move on. And Jess had done that. She'd put the "what ifs" aside, learned to deal with her pain and then established a new career—and a new life. No, it wasn't totally "normal" yet. She still didn't sleep well. She didn't eat enough. And despite the support of her family, a deep, aching loneliness was still her constant companion. But no one knew that. In fact, few people outside her family would ever guess the trauma she'd been through. So yes, she had moved on. And she'd felt good about the progress she'd made.

Until now.

Because Scott's return had completely unsettled her, resurrecting doubts and emotions and questions that she thought had been laid to rest long ago. It had been easy to hate him, to blame him for everything, to think of him as cold and uncaring, when he was miles away. It was a whole lot harder when he stood three feet in front of her, his eyes filled with anguish and regret.

His physical presence also made her remember all too clearly the love and intimacy they had shared before ambition distracted his attention from the things that really mattered. It was one thing to dream about those things from the past, and a different thing altogether to have the subject of those dreams stand only an outstretched hand away in the present.

And she certainly hadn't expected him to still love her. Not after the hateful things she'd said to him when Elizabeth died. Not after the cold, bitter note she'd sent him following the accident. Not after years of ignoring his letters. Nor had she expected his gentleness, or the quiet calm that seemed to reflect an inner peace and an acceptance of the past, as if he'd come to grips with what he'd done and found a way to live with it.

Her chaotic emotions, her sudden doubt and uncertainty, made her wonder whether she'd been deluding herself all along. Had she really dealt with the past, or simply ignored it, focusing on the *events* while burying the real *issues* deep in the recesses of her mind and heart unresolved—and still raw? If she had truly resolved her issues and put the past behind her, wouldn't she feel some of the quiet calm, the acceptance, that she'd seen in the depths of Scott's eyes? And if she had truly written Scott off, hated him as deeply as she'd convinced herself she did, wouldn't she have been able to sustain her righteous anger and dismiss him without a second thought? Wouldn't she have been able to ignore the love and regret in his eyes?

Wearily Jess let her head drop back against the upholstered chair. The answer to those questions was obvious: yes. But in reality, she felt far from calm. She hadn't been able to dismiss him. And she hadn't been able to ignore the emotions she saw in his eyes. Like it or not, Scott's presence had disrupted her carefully reconstructed existence.

For more than three years, Jess had suppressed memories of the life she'd shared with Scott. But now she could no longer keep them at bay. So with a resigned sigh she let them flow.

Jess thought back to their first encounter, in a business meeting. They'd done no more than shake hands and say a few words, but the spark that leapt between them had made her nerve endings sizzle and left her stunned. He had looked equally dazed. So she hadn't been in the least surprised when he'd called the next day and asked her out.

From their very first date, Jess had known that Scott was the man she would marry. And when she'd walked down the aisle with him a year and a half later, her heart overflowing with love, she'd looked forward with joy to the life they would build together as husband and wife.

The first few years of their marriage had more than lived up to her expectations, she recalled wistfully. They cooked together, laughing over exotic new recipes. They gardened, a passion they both shared. They took weekend hiking trips. And when Elizabeth came, bringing a new joy and closeness to their relationship, Jess willingly gave up her public relations job to be a full-time mother. It was a decision she and Scott made jointly and with absolute conviction. Her joy seemed complete.

But as Scott began to climb the corporate ladder, things started to change. Slowly at first. In manageable increments. A late night at the office here. A missed family event there. Jess could handle those. She understood that there would be occasional conflicts between work and personal life. What she *didn't* realize was that those minor changes were only previews of the major ones to come. Because Scott had been "noticed" by the right people. His talents had been recognized. And as a result, career demands increased. "Rising young executives," it seemed, were expected to put their jobs first. Always. Period.

Jess tried to cope with Scott's increased absences and his growing distraction. She watched with alarm as his job became the center of his life. Between his cell phone, e-mail and pager he was never able to get away from the office. She kept telling herself that in time the demands would ease. But as the months, then years, went by and the pace only intensified, she realized that things would never change unless *Scott* changed them.

So Jess tried to talk to him about it. Repeatedly. But the conversations always followed the same script.

"What do you want me to do about it, Jess?" Scott would say impatiently. "In this business, if you're not on the fast track, you're not on *any* track. And I can't afford to be without a job. I'm the sole breadwinner. Which is fine. We agreed to that. But I do feel more pressure now to provide us with a good living.''

"Good is one thing, Scott," she'd reply earnestly. "But I don't need that huge new house you've been talking about. Or the new car. Or a diamond bracelet for Christmas. I'm perfectly happy with simple things. Maybe you could change agencies, find a less demanding job. One that would give us more time to spend together.''

He would frown then, the conflict in his eyes apparent. "I know I haven't been around as much as you'd like, Jess. But people don't just walk away from jobs like this."

"Why not?"

The question was always met with a sigh of exasperation. "I worked too hard to give all this up now."

"Give what up? The country club membership? The designer suits? Is that what you're talking about?''

"Is there something wrong with those things?" he'd ask defensively.

"No. Only when they come at the expense of other, more important things.''

"I'm doing the best I can to balance everything, Jess. I'll just have to try harder, I guess.''

And that's where the conversation would always end. In a stalemate.

Two years into that lifestyle and after numerous dead-end conversations on the subject, Jess began to notice another disturbing change in Scott's behavior. He'd always enjoyed a glass of wine with a special dinner, a beer while cutting the grass on the weekend.

But now he went for the harder stuff. A gin and tonic became his standard way to unwind at the end of a long day. And at social gatherings he drank far more than was prudent. It was one more worry for Jess to add to her growing list.

But there were good times, too. Scott was a wonderful father—when he was home. He never looked more relaxed or happy than when he was playing with Elizabeth. And she adored him, reaching out her small chubby arms to him and laughing with glee when he appeared. They had good moments as a couple, as well. In the small hours of the morning he would sometimes curl up behind her, stroke her body and whisper words of love that made her heart ache with tenderness—and with a bittersweet pang for the days when making time for love had been his first priority.

And then tragedy struck. The death of her beloved daughter. Bitterness. Recriminations. The end of their marriage in everything but name. The death of her dream for a happily-ever-after life.

Jess felt a tear trickle down her cheek, and she reached up to wipe it away. With an unsteady hand she raised the mug to her lips and took a sip.

But her tea had grown cold.

Just like her life.

"You look tired, honey. Are you feeling okay?"

Jess glanced at her mother. She usually enjoyed the weekly evening with her parents, but she'd dreaded tonight's dinner. She'd done her best to camouflage the dark circles under her eyes, the result of several almost sleepless nights, but obviously her makeup skills hadn't been up to the task.

"It's been busy at the office," she hedged.

"I'm looking forward to the iris show," Frank remarked.

"So am I," Jess said with a smile. Taking her parents to see the gardens when the irises were at their peak, followed by an elegant brunch in one of the downtown hotels, had become an eagerly anticipated annual outing.

"Speaking of flowers, I need to order some mulch for the rose beds. And I think I lost my Mr. Lincoln this winter. I'll have to replace that as soon as the shipments come in." He turned to Jess. "I'm planning to extend the back garden and add a few more bushes this year."

She smiled. Her father's rose garden was a neighborhood legend. "How many do you have now, Dad?"

"Forty-five."

"I don't know why you even bother going down to the botanical garden. You have your own right here."

He looked pleased. "Mostly roses, though. I like to look at all the other flowers, too."

"So have you been working longer hours?" Clare asked Jess, doggedly returning to her earlier line of questioning.

Jess toyed with the food on her plate, and took a deep breath. She might as well tell them about Scott's visit. After all, they were all adults. They could discuss the situation rationally. "Yes. And not sleeping very well for the past few days. Scott came by on Saturday.''

Her father stared at her in stunned silence for a moment, then threw his napkin on the table and stood. "That's it. I'm calling John Kane. We'll put a stop to this."

So much for rational discussion, Jess thought ruefully. This was the reaction she'd been afraid of. "I don't think that's necessary, Dad."

He planted his fists on his hips. "Are you telling me that you're not upset by these contacts?"

"No. But he'll get the message eventually."

"He'll get it a lot faster if he gets slapped with a restraining order."

He'd also get in trouble. Probably big trouble, Jess figured. She doubted the criminal justice system showed much mercy to newly released prisoners who were accused of harassment. And after looking into his eyes, she just couldn't do that to him.

"Let it go for now, Dad," she said quietly. "I'll think about it if this keeps up."

Her father studied her appraisingly. "What did he say to you?"

She shrugged. "Not much. Just that he was sorry."

Frank snorted. "It's a little late for that."

"I told him the same thing."

"Did you also tell him to leave you alone?"

"More or less. I shut the door in his face."

"I don't like this, Jess," Clare said, clearly worried. "It's been a hard few years for you. You don't need to have your life disrupted again."

Jess didn't disagree. The trouble was, her life was already disrupted.

When she didn't respond, Frank spoke again. "Your mother's right, Jess. You've been through enough."

Jess looked at her parents. They'd always been overly protective of their only daughter. And while she deeply valued their support and understanding and unqualified love, this was a decision she had to make on her own. She'd been affected by Scott's return in ways she didn't quite understand. And until she did, until she made sense of her chaotic emotions and thoughts, she was reluctant to take any action.

"I appreciate your concern. But I want to give this a little time," she said firmly.

There was silence around the table for a moment, and then Clare spoke. "It's her decision, Frank. She'll let us know if she wants us to step in."

Jess sent her mother a grateful look, then transferred her gaze to her father. He frowned in disapproval and seemed poised to make another comment. But after a moment he silently took his seat instead, confining his response to a single sentence.

"I hope you know what you're doing," he said shortly.

So did she, Jess thought with a sigh.

"The welcoming committee's here!"

Scott grinned at Karen, who stood on the other side of his door bearing a pie carrier in one hand and a plate of brownies in the other. "I'm salivating already. I haven't had anything home cooked in years."

"There's more," she called over her shoulder as she

sailed past. "The cooler in the trunk is filled with lasagna, meat loaf and a bunch of other stuff. Can you grab that while I take these to the kitchen?"

Scott did as requested, returning to find Karen surveying his apartment with a frown, her hands planted on her hips, her lips compressed into a thin line. Here it comes, he thought resignedly as he deposited the cooler on the kitchen floor. He took a deep breath and braced himself before turning toward her

"I appreciate all this food, sis. More than you know. But you didn't need to go to so much trouble. It must have taken you days to make all this."

"I'm glad I did. I just checked your freezer and your cabinets. Corn flakes, bread, instant rice, instant mashed potatoes, canned stew, eggs. Is that what you've been living on?"

"It beats prison fare," he replied lightly. "Was the drive down okay?"

"It was fine. But I'm not through talking about you yet." Her gaze swept over the apartment before returning to him, and she folded her arms across her chest. "This isn't acceptable, Scott."

"I warned you it wasn't the Ritz."

"It isn't even a cut-rate motel," she shot back.

"It's good enough for now."

"There was a lovely guest room waiting for you in my house. There still is."

"I need to be here, Karen," he said quietly.

She looked at him in silence for a few moments. "Because of Jess."

"Yes."

She sighed resignedly. "Well, I'm not going to argue with you about that. It would be a lost cause. But I'm not happy about this,'' she said with a sweeping gesture around the tiny apartment.

"I didn't think you would be.''

"Is this really all you can afford?''

"For now.''

"Does Jess know how you live?''

"No.''

She bit her lip. "Look, Scott, I know you signed everything over to her when you went to prison, but don't you think you deserve *something*—just enough to give you a stake to get started again?''

"No,'' he replied flatly.

Karen shook her head in exasperation. "Okay, I'm not going to argue with you about this. Yet. Put on your coat. We're going out to dinner. My treat.''

Scott frowned. "But there's plenty of food here.''

"That's for you. After I go back.'' When he started to protest, she held up her hand. "Not open for discussion. Besides, after the long drive down here I deserve a night away from the kitchen.''

Scott shook his head bemusedly. "Are you this bossy at home?''

She shrugged. "I happen to be a strong-willed woman.''

"Bossy,'' he reiterated.

"Assertive,'' she corrected.

"Stubborn, too.''

"If you keep insulting me I just might pack up my food and go home,'' she threatened.

Scott held up his hands in capitulation and then

reached for his jacket. "Heaven forbid! You win," he said with a chuckle.

"I'm glad you see the light," she said smugly.

Not until they were seated in the quiet restaurant and had placed their orders did Karen once again bring up the subject of Scott's wife. "So tell me how things are going with Jess."

"They aren't."

"Are you giving up?"

"No. Regrouping. Trying to figure out how to break through the wall she's built between us." Suddenly Scott's eyes grew thoughtful as he studied Karen. "Hey, I just had an idea," he said slowly.

She gazed at him suspiciously. "I don't like that look in your eyes."

He ignored her comment. "Maybe *you* could convince her to talk to me."

Karen stared at him. "I haven't spoken with her in years," she protested. "Why would she listen to me?"

"Because Jess always liked you. And she won't hold *my* mistakes against *you*. I'm willing to bet that she'll at least be polite." He sighed and raked his fingers through his hair. "Look, I hate to ask you to do this. And I don't know if it will work," he admitted. "But I'm willing to try anything at this point. She's shut me out both times I've tried to contact her. I need someone to run interference for me."

Karen waited while their food was placed in front of them, her brow furrowed. "I'm not into confrontation, Scott."

He tried to smile. "You could have fooled me. You don't cut me any slack."

She made a face. "Very funny. You're my brother. That's different."

He looked at her steadily. "I know it's asking a lot, Karen. You've already gone above and beyond. But this means a lot to me."

Karen was silent for a moment, then she sighed deeply and picked up her fork. "I'll think about it, okay? Now eat your steak before it gets cold."

Jess glanced toward the door in surprise, then at her watch. Her pizza order had arrived in record time. Which was okay. For the first time in several days she was actually hungry. She reached for her wallet, then headed toward the foyer.

"You guys get faster all the..." Her voice trailed off as she stared at the petite, dark-haired woman facing her on the other side of the door. Scott's sister.

Karen nervously hitched up her shoulder purse and offered a tentative smile. "Hello, Jess."

Instead of responding, Jess glanced behind Karen, her gaze darting into the shadows of the deepening dusk.

"I'm alone."

Jess's gaze swung back to Karen, who looked as uneasy and uncomfortable as Jess felt. "Do you have a few minutes to talk?" Karen asked.

"I don't really think we have anything to say to each other, Karen." She was amazed at how cool and controlled she sounded, considering her insides felt like gelatin.

"I won't take much of your time."

Jess didn't budge. "Did Scott ask you to come here?"

Karen hesitated, then nodded. "Yes."

"Look, Karen, I don't have anything against you. In fact, I always liked you. But nothing you say will make any difference. I don't want Scott in my life. Period. I've made that pretty clear both times he's contacted me. I don't know what else I have to do."

Karen took a deep breath and held her ground. "How about five minutes?" she persisted. "That's all I ask."

Short of closing the door in Karen's face, Jess was faced with no option but to grant her request. Besides, she didn't want to hurt Karen. Or be rude. The woman had always been kind to her, and the two couples had shared some very good times. What could it hurt to give her five minutes? In fact, it might help. If Karen saw how resolute Jess was, maybe she would carry that message back to Scott and discourage him from further contact. It was worth a try.

Jess stepped aside and opened the door. "All right. Five minutes."

Karen moved past her, and Jess nodded toward the living room. "Would you like something to drink?"

"No, thanks," Karen replied as she settled on the edge of the couch. Jess perched on the arm of a chair across from her, folded her arms and waited.

Karen gripped her purse and took a steadying breath. "Look, Jess, I really don't want to be here. But I love Scott. I've seen what he's gone through these last few years. And I want to help him. He's had a really tough time."

"Forgive me if I can't feel too sorry for him."

Karen seemed momentarily taken aback by the sarcasm in Jess's voice. "I don't mean to imply you haven't, too, Jess. But prison is hell."

"So is tragedy. And loneliness. And grief. You don't have to be behind bars to taste hell," she replied tersely.

Karen nodded. "I realize that. But in addition to everything else, Scott also carried a heavy burden of guilt. He lost the two things he loved most in the world—Elizabeth and you. And it was his own fault. He lived with the anguish alone, day after day, locked in an eight-by-eight cell, with no one to talk to, no one to comfort him, no support system. It...it almost killed him."

For a moment Jess seemed taken aback. "What do you mean?"

"He wanted to die, Jess," Karen said quietly. "I came to visit him every month, and for the first year I was afraid every time I left that he would...do something. He lost forty pounds, and his hands shook all the time. And he always had this hopeless look in his eyes, even though he tried to act normal when I was there. But I know him too well. And he was far from normal. I worried every day."

Jess eyed her skeptically. "He looks fine now."

"He's better," Karen conceded. "But hardly fine. He believes there are unresolved issues between the two of you. And he'd like a chance to address them. That's why he wants to see you."

Jess couldn't argue about the unresolved issues. Not after spending too many sleepless nights thinking about the situation. But she didn't need to talk with Scott to deal with them. She'd work through them eventually. On her own. As she did everything these days. Her eyes grew cool and she shook her head.

"I don't think so, Karen."

For a moment Karen studied the woman across from her. Jess was almost like a stranger. An unhappy, unreachable stranger, whose eyes reflected disillusion and bitterness. "You've changed, Jess," Karen said quietly.

"Haven't we all."

"Yes. And that includes Scott. I wish you'd give him a chance to prove that to you."

Jess stood, her face impassive. "If he's changed, I'm glad. But that doesn't bring back Elizabeth. It doesn't bring back the judge who was killed. All it brings back is the pain. If he really cares for me, he'll leave me alone. I would appreciate it if you'd tell him that."

Karen hesitated a moment, then stood and walked toward the door. She paused at the threshold to look back at the other woman, her eyes sad. "I'm sorry I bothered you, Jess. And I hope you don't regret this decision. I have a feeling that you're making a big mistake."

As Karen walked away, Jess frowned and slowly closed the door. Was she making a mistake? Or was she being wise?

She didn't have a clue.

And when her pizza arrived a few minutes later, she realized that her appetite had vanished—just like her peace of mind.

* * *

"I'm sorry, Scott," Karen concluded with a sigh as she finished the report on her visit with Jess.

Scott tried to hide his disappointment. He'd known all along that it was foolish to hope that Karen's visit would make a difference. And it wasn't her fault that Jess had been unreceptive. "Don't be. You did your best. I knew it was a long shot."

Karen wrapped her hands around her mug and stared into the dark depths of her coffee. "Jess has changed a lot," she said carefully.

"Yeah. I know. She's way too thin. And too tense. And much more high-strung."

Karen nodded. "True. But she's different in other ways, too."

Scott frowned. "What do you mean?"

Karen shrugged. "I don't know, exactly. Jess used to be so open and full of joy. Now it's like she's shut down. Like there's no way to reach her. She has such bitterness and anger...." Karen shook her head in dismay. "Frankly, I don't know what it will take to get through to her."

"There has to be a way," Scott said resolutely.

Karen looked at him steadily. "And if there isn't?"

"I'm not willing to consider that yet."

"You know, sometimes people are physically hurt so badly that they can't be saved," Karen said softly. "I think the same is true of some relationships."

Scott rested his elbows on his knees and dropped his face into his hands. After a moment he drew a long shuddering breath, and when he looked at Karen a bit of light had gone out of his eyes.

"I'm not giving up."

"She doesn't want to see you, Scott."

"I respect that. But I believe that God is with me on this. Because I know, in my heart, that the marriage He blessed was meant to go on. And not just in name."

Karen's eyes were filled with compassion when she looked at him. "I hope you're right, Scott. But I think it will take a miracle."

"I survived three years of hell, Karen," he said, his gaze locked on hers. "I believe in miracles."

She had no rebuttal to that. "I wish I could help."

"You can. Pray."

"I already do. Every day."

"Then keep it up."

Because he knew he would need all the prayers he could get to bring about *this* miracle.

Chapter Four

 ❧

At first glance, Jess wasn't sure. It *looked* like Scott from the back. In fact, as she studied the distant figure more closely, it looked enough like him to make her step falter. But surely she was wrong. Why would Scott be planting bushes in front of the hospital? she wondered in confusion.

Suddenly the man turned, and her suspicion became reality. It *was* Scott, she realized as her heart skipped a beat. For a moment he seemed as taken aback by her presence as she had been by his. Then he slowly set his shovel aside and walked toward her.

Jess thought about turning away, fleeing in the opposite direction. But she wasn't going to spend her life running. Since Scott lived in St. Louis, there was always a chance their paths would cross. She'd have to learn to accept that. And deal with it in a mature way. Which she was perfectly capable of doing, she told herself determinedly. After all, her first encounters with him had been upsetting only because they'd been so unexpected. Now that the initial shock had worn off, she was better prepared to deal with him.

Scott stopped a few feet away. Despite the chill in the air, he wore only jeans and a sweatshirt. There was a streak of dirt on his forehead, and he looked tired, Jess realized. As if he hadn't been getting enough sleep. The unfamiliar lines she'd noticed on his face at their first meeting seemed a bit deeper, too. Or maybe they were just more apparent in the harsh noonday sun, which also highlighted the sprinkling of silver at his temples. For the first time, Jess was consciously aware of the physical evidence of the hell Karen had said he'd endured. But she steeled herself against it. He had no corner on anguish, she thought harshly. Her lips compressed into a thin, unreceptive line and she stared at him mutely. Since he'd approached her, she waited for him to speak first.

Scott jammed his hands into his pockets, realizing that the ball was in his court. But he had no idea what to say. He was still trying to recover from the shock of seeing Jess so unexpectedly. Though his feet had automatically carried him in her direction, his brain hadn't yet kicked into gear. So for a moment he just drank in the sight of her. Her honey-gold, shoulder-length hair was pulled back at her nape with a barrette, and she wore tailored black slacks and a forest-green jacket with a black velvet collar. His gaze lingered at her neck, where a gold choker glinted in the sunlight and a rapid pulse beat in the hollow of her throat. Was she nervous, he wondered? Angry? About to let him have it—or about to give him a chance to plead his case?

Hoping her eyes might hold a clue, his gaze moved on, past her lips, past the dark shadows that indicated she, too, had been finding sleep elusive. But when his gaze reached her eyes, their green depths were cool and shuttered—and very unreadable. He'd just have to wing it, he realized. With an effort he swallowed past the lump in his throat and struggled to find his voice.

"Hello, Jess."

Her eyes were aloof as her gaze swept over his dirt-stained clothes. "What are you doing here?"

"Working." When she frowned, he nodded toward a landscaping truck off to the side. "I work for that company."

Jess's frown deepened. With Scott's experience, she'd just assumed that he was back in the marketing game. It had never occurred to her he would be working as a manual laborer. That sort of job would have been completely unacceptable to the Scott she remembered, who had come to value designer suits and power lunches, who had liked starched shirts and clean fingernails. It didn't make any sense.

Of course, it was no concern of hers. She really didn't care what he was doing. Yet she couldn't stop the question that sprang to her lips. "What happened to marketing?"

He shrugged. "Ex-cons can't be picky. Besides, I don't have the stomach for it anymore. Or the heart. And I wanted an outdoor job."

She almost asked why, then thought better of it. The answer was obvious. If you'd spent three years of your life confined in the eight-by-eight cell Karen had described, she doubted a desk job in an eight-by-eight office would be very appealing.

"Why are *you* here?" he asked, interrupting her thoughts.

"Visiting a friend who just had surgery," she replied distractedly, still mulling over his response to her question. "I ran over on my lunch hour."

"And what are you doing these days, Jess?"

Jess snapped back to attention. The question was asked gently, with genuine interest. But she saw no point in prolonging the conversation. She glanced at her watch. "I'm running late. Goodbye, Scott." And with that she brushed past him, leaving a faint, appealing fragrance in her wake.

Scott watched her walk away and slowly let out his breath. After Karen's visit, he'd prayed for guidance about how best to approach Jess. He'd also talked with Reverend Young, who had wisely reminded him that patience was his friend in this endeavor and that the Lord would show him the way in His time—not in Scott's time. So Scott had put his faith in God. And now that faith had been rewarded. Best of all, Jess hadn't appeared upset. Or angry. And she'd actually said more than three words to him. Yes, the conversation had been strained and awkward. And no, she hadn't exactly been friendly. But it was a start, he thought with renewed hope.

For her part, Jess was more shaken by the encounter than she'd let on. Her heart was hammering in her chest, and as she punched the elevator button she realized that her hand was trembling. But at least she'd managed to remain poised and in control during their brief exchange, she congratulated herself. Her shock at coming upon Scott had been far less dramatic than at their first two encounters. In fact, she was more shocked by his job than by his presence. Manual labor seemed somehow inappropriate for a man of Scott's intelligence and abilities and experience. Why had he settled for such a job? There had to be higher-level jobs, even for an ex-con, that wouldn't require him to spend his whole day in a confined office. Yet he'd chosen to be a laborer. Jess frowned, recalling Karen's comment that Scott had changed. His job choice certainly seemed to bear that out, she acknowledged begrudgingly.

But if she was puzzled by Scott's choice of work, she felt good about her reaction to him. She hadn't fled, despite the temptation to do so. She'd kept her cool. She hadn't been swayed by the warmth in his eyes.

And the next time she saw him—if there was a next time—it would be even easier to walk away undisturbed, she thought with satisfaction.

Jess pulled into a parking place and glanced at her watch in frustration. If she hadn't been running late this morning, she wouldn't have walked out the door without the report she needed to present this afternoon. Skipping lunch to run home and retrieve it simply added to the pressure of an already stressful day.

Jess was halfway down the walk toward her condo when she noticed the man sitting on the ground, his back against a tree, his long legs stretched out in front of him. He was at right angles to her, engrossed in a book, and a crumpled brown paper sack and empty soda can lying on its side were beside him.

Jess's headlong rush slowed, then came to an abrupt halt. It was Scott again! Less than a week after she'd run into him at the hospital, she realized incredulously. The last encounter she had written off to chance. But you could stretch coincidence only so far. If he was going to start staking out her home, then she'd have no choice but to follow her father's advice and have a restraining order issued, she thought angrily.

Just then, as if sensing her presence, Scott looked toward her. Though his surprised reaction momentarily let some of the air out of her theory of a deliberate setup, she still couldn't buy pure chance. The odds against them running into each other twice in only a few days were too great. Taking a deep breath, she strode toward him.

"What are you doing here?" she demanded.

He closed his book and rose in one lithe movement. But instead of the defensive reaction she expected, his posture was relaxed, his gaze warm. A smile tugged at the corner of his mouth in the endearing way she had always loved, and she suddenly found it difficult to breathe. "Didn't we have this same conversation at the hospital?"

She folded her arms across her chest. "You didn't answer my question."

"I'm working." He shifted his book to the other hand and pointed to the Lawson Landscaping truck in the parking lot—which she'd have noticed if she hadn't been so rushed, she realized—then nodded toward a shovel and a flat of begonias a few feet away. "Now it's my turn. What are *you* doing here?"

She ignored his teasing tone. "I live here, remember?"

"I mean what are you doing here at lunchtime? We're always long gone before the eight-to-five crowd gets home."

She frowned in confusion. "You've worked here before?"

"Several times. Lawson has the groundskeeping contract for this complex."

The implications of his reply slowly sank in. He'd been in her neighborhood on more than one occasion. And he had made no attempt to contact her. So much for her father's harassment theory, she thought wryly.

"So what brings you home at lunchtime?" he repeated.

"I forgot a report that I need this afternoon."

A slow smile spread over Scott's face. "The Lord really does work in mysterious ways," he said softly.

She frowned again. "What's that supposed to mean?"

"I've been praying for our paths to cross again, Jess."

"This is just a coincidence," she scoffed.

"Oh ye of little faith."

The truth of the remark, said partly in jest, stung. "Since when have you gotten so holy?" she lashed out. "I seem to recall having to drag you to church when we were..." She stopped abruptly. "Well, a long time ago."

Suddenly his face grew serious. "I've changed,

Jess. My faith is the main reason I survived the last few years.''

She stared at him. ''Do you really expect me to believe that?''

''It's the truth,'' he said simply. ''You of all people should understand that. Your faith was always important to you. Now I know why.''

But I don't, she thought silently. *Not anymore.* Her spoken words, however, were different. ''Look, I don't have time for philosophical discussions,'' she said irritably. ''I'm running late. You can believe whatever you want about these two meetings. I call it chance. Bad luck. Whatever. And I think it's highly unlikely to happen again. In fact, I hope with all my heart that it doesn't. Goodbye, Scott.''

She lifted her chin and headed toward her condo. Though she purposely didn't look at him again, the title of the book he held somehow seemed to jump out at her as she passed. And for a moment her step faltered. It was the Holy Bible, she realized in astonishment.

As she picked up her pace once again, she suddenly—and much to her surprise—realized that she was envious. Because Scott had clearly found in *his* faith what she'd always claimed to have in *hers.* Trust in the Lord. A belief that no matter what happened, He was always with us. And a deep conviction that if we turned to Him for help, if we admitted our faults and asked for forgiveness, He would stand with us and welcome us home.

When she'd first seen Scott, she'd been struck by

the deep inner peace in his eyes. Now she knew the source.

It was ironic, she thought with a bittersweet pang. In Scott's adversity, when he'd felt most abandoned, the Lord had taken him in. Just the opposite had happened with her. In her adversity, she had walked away from her faith. Because she believed the Lord had abandoned her.

For the first time since Elizabeth's death, Jess acknowledged that the loss of her faith had made her the poorer. But she had no idea how to rebuild it. Or even if she wanted to. Because that would mean once more putting her trust in the Lord. And at this point in her life, she had very little trust to give.

To anyone.

"The garden's coming along beautifully, Scott."

Scott wiped his forehead on his sleeve as he gazed with satisfaction at the plantings that were transforming the area around the just-finished gazebo into a meditation garden. Dogwoods, Japanese maples, azaleas, boxwoods, lilies, hydrangeas, irises and banks of perennials now framed the slightly elevated natural wood structure. The layout was pleasing to the eye, and the plants had been chosen to provide a season-long display of color. "Thanks. I'm happy with the way it turned out," Scott concurred. "In a year or two, when everything is really established, this will be a lovely spot."

"It looks pretty good to me right now. And the board agrees. I'm sure they'll thank you officially, but in the meantime they wanted me to pass on their compliments.''

"It was no big deal,'' Scott replied with a shrug. "I had the time, and it was a good chance for me to test my landscape-design skills.''

Reverend Young smiled. "Well, if this was a test, you get an A." He held up a sack. "Mrs. Wagner dropped off some of her famous white-chocolate-chip macadamia-nut cookies. Think you could help me get rid of a few?''

Scott grinned. "I think that could be arranged." He laid his shovel aside and wiped his hands on his slacks before following the minister to the gazebo.

"Looks like spring's really arrived,'' the minister said as he settled onto one of the benches that rimmed the inside of the gazebo. He retrieved two cans of soda from the sack and handed one to Scott.

Scott took a long sip, then nodded. "That's for sure. Things are hopping at Seth's.''

"I'll bet. Everything okay with the job?''

"Seems to be. Seth doesn't say much, but he's put me in charge of the crew a couple of times when the chief was sick. I take that as a good sign.''

"I agree. Apartment okay?''

Scott smiled. "Not according to my sister. But it's fine for now.''

"Still taking the bus everywhere?''

Scott reached for a cookie. "Yes. But I must admit that I'll be glad to get a car. I figure in another month or two, I should be able to swing it.''

"I'd be more than happy to loan you the—''

"No.'' Scott cut him off firmly, then softened his

tone. "I appreciate the offer, Reverend. But I want to do this myself."

"It's okay to accept *some* help, Scott."

"I need it more on another front," he replied with a sigh.

"Jess?"

"Mmm-hmm."

"How are things going?"

He shrugged. "I guess there's a little progress. We've run into each other a couple of times, and she's actually spoken to me."

"That's a start."

"Barely."

"Hang in there. And keep praying."

"I plan to."

The minister took a sip of his soda, then carefully placed the can on the wooden bench. "I'd like to ask a favor of you, Scott."

Scott looked at the man who had helped him find his way back to the Lord, who had given him a reason to live again. There was no way he could ever repay him for his kindness and caring. No favor would be too great. "Name it," he said promptly.

"Well, a group of area churches will be sponsoring a one-day retreat in a few weeks. The title is 'Coping with Adversity—Ask and You Shall Receive.' Some of the clergy will be giving talks and leading discussions, but we're also looking for people who are willing to give a firsthand account of how, in the face of tragedy, their faith helped them turn their lives around. You have a remarkable story to tell, Scott. We'd be honored if you'd share it."

Scott stared at Reverend Young. Bare his soul in front of a group of strangers? He couldn't even imagine it! He'd never been the kind of guy who went around talking about his feelings—even to people he *knew*. Besides, he was no role model. His journey to faith had been a painful one, fraught with doubt and dead ends and despair. Hardly the stuff of inspiration. Yet he owed so much to Reverend Young. He hated to say no.

The minister smiled understandingly. "I can see you're surprised by my request."

"That's too mild a word." He raked his fingers through his hair and stared out at the placid waters of the pond for a moment before speaking. "It's not that I don't want to help, Reverend," he said slowly. "But I've made a lot of mistakes. I'm not sure I'm the best example to hold up to people. There are a lot of things I'm still struggling with. And even though I do have hope, I'm not where I want to be yet."

"That's precisely the point, Scott. Your hope will be inspiring to many people who are also struggling. And as for mistakes…that makes you human. Someone people can relate to. All of us have made mistakes, all of us have challenges in our lives. Generally not as big as the ones you've faced, thank God. But that's why your story will resonate with people. If you could find your way to God despite the problems that you had to shoulder, it gives all of us hope that we can do the same with our lesser struggles." He paused for a moment, then delivered his powerful closing argument. "Your witness could make the difference in some life teetering on the edge of despair, Scott."

Put that way, Scott realized that he was left with little choice. He had vowed to make his faith the center of his life, and here was a perfect opportunity to give something back to the Lord, who had sustained him through his trials. But it wouldn't be easy. He had never been comfortable sharing painful experiences. Even in the best days of his marriage he'd held back some of his doubts and fears from Jess, feeling that such an admission would somehow diminish him, make him less strong. Now he recognized that attitude, which still lingered, for what it was—a sin of pride. Funny. He thought the past three years had stripped away all remnants of his pride. Clearly, patience wasn't the only virtue he needed to work on, he acknowledged ruefully. Humility was right up there, too.

Scott took a deep breath. "You make it hard to say no. But this won't be easy for me, Reverend."

The minister laid his hand on Scott's shoulder. "Not much worth doing is, Scott," he said kindly. "But remember that when we have faith, we never do anything alone. And that knowledge should always give us the courage to carry on."

"Hey, Skip. What's up?"

Jess smiled at her brother's voice and headed toward a comfortable chair, switching the portable phone to her other hand. "Are you ever going to stop calling me that?" she complained good-naturedly.

"Why should I?"

"Because I don't skip anymore, for one thing. And for another, that nickname is too childlike for an adult woman."

"What's wrong with being childlike?" he countered. "Innocence and trust are good things. And you're never too old to skip."

"I disagree on all counts. If you have the first two, you get hurt. And my skipping days are over."

"More's the pity."

"So how are you enjoying Japan?" she asked, deliberately changing the subject.

"Okay, okay. I can take a hint. Japan was great."

"Was?"

"Yep. We wrapped things up and I came home a week early. I just got in a couple of hours ago, in fact. With a major case of jet lag," he added, stifling a yawn. "Let me tell you, fourteen hours on a plane is *not* my idea of a great time."

"So why aren't you sleeping?"

"That's the next item on my agenda. But first I want to hear about you. Why didn't you tell me Scott was out?"

Jess frowned. "How did you know?"

"Mom let it slip. So why didn't you tell me? I just talked to you last week."

"Because it doesn't matter."

"Yeah?"

"Yeah."

"That's not what Mom said."

"What do you mean?"

"She said you're rattled."

"I'm not rattled."

"You sound rattled."

"I'm not rattled!" she repeated more emphatically.

"Okay, okay! You're not rattled. Fine. So how is he?"

"How would I know?"

"Mom said you've seen him."

Jess sighed. "What else has Mom told you?"

"That there's talk of a restraining order. Is that true?"

"The talk part is. I haven't done anything about it yet."

"Is Scott bugging you?"

"Not really. He called once. And stopped by. Then he sent his sister to try and convince me to talk with him."

"Did she succeed?"

"No."

There was silence for a moment. "Do you want some advice?"

"No. But why do I think that won't stop you from giving it?" she said resignedly.

"Because you know me too well. Listen, would it hurt to talk to him, Jess? The man just spent three years in prison. Behind bars. Caged up like an animal. He's had a lot of time to think about what happened. Maybe he has some things he'd like to say to you."

"Maybe I don't want to hear them."

"Maybe you should."

Jess gave a frustrated sigh. "Nothing he can say will change anything, Mark. Our marriage is over, except in name. Elizabeth is dead. The life I knew with Scott is gone. I've started over. I see no point in rehashing old hurts."

"So how are you sleeping these days?"

At the abrupt change of subject, Jess frowned in confusion. "What?"

"How are you sleeping?"

"What has that got to do with anything?"

"Maybe a lot. Unresolved issues can prey on the mind."

"I don't have unresolved issues," she replied with more confidence than she felt.

"I don't buy that," he said bluntly. "I never have. I think you need to talk to Scott and work through this. Look, Jess, I know you've vilified him in your mind. But you loved him once. Doesn't that count for anything?"

"No," she said flatly.

Mark sighed. "Frankly, I don't buy *that,* either. I know how much you two were in love. At the risk of getting sappy, it was almost magic to watch you together. But putting all that aside for a minute, I knew Scott, too. I'm not saying he was perfect. Or that what he did wasn't wrong. But he was never a *bad* man. In fact, he had great integrity and principle. And he clearly believes that there are unresolved issues between the two of you. Deep in your heart, I think you feel the same way."

"Since when have you become a psychiatrist?" Jess said sarcastically.

He refused to be baited by her tone. "I think it's just common sense," he replied matter-of-factly.

"You're forgetting one thing, Mark." A tremor of anger and pain rippled through her voice, and she took a steadying breath. "Scott killed my daughter. And I can never forget that."

There was silence for a moment, and when Mark spoke again his voice was sober. "I understand that, Jess. But that doesn't mean you can't forgive."

Jess drew in a sharp breath, feeling almost as if she'd been slapped. "You expect me to forgive him?" she asked incredulously.

"I leave that up to you. But holding on to hate doesn't seem very productive. In fact, it usually holds us *back*. Sometimes forgiving is the only way to move on."

Jess had no response to that. Because, though her mind denied the truth of Mark's observation, her heart wasn't so sure.

"Are you still there?" Mark asked when the silence lengthened.

"I'm here," she replied stiffly.

"Listen, I'm sorry if I overstepped. But I care about you, Jess. I know talking to Scott would be difficult, but it also might free you once and for all from the anger that you've carried all these years."

Jess took a deep breath, and when she spoke she sounded weary—and spent. "I know you mean well, Mark. But this is something I have to deal with myself. And at this point I just don't want to talk to Scott."

"Will you at least think about it?"

She hesitated. "Maybe."

"Then enough said. Listen, I have *got* to get some rest. I'll call you again in a few days, okay?"

"Yeah."

"Take care, Skip."

A smile tugged at the corners of her mouth as the line went dead. Mark was incorrigible. But he was also smart. The "book" smarts she'd always known about, of course. You didn't get a Harvard MBA without superior intelligence. But his insights into her psyche surprised her.

Jess's grin faded and her face grew serious. Mark hadn't said much about the tragedy during Scott's imprisonment, and the few times he'd broached the subject she'd cut him off. So he'd let it rest. Until today. Now that Scott was out, and making his intentions clear that he'd like to talk with her, Mark had apparently become a man with a mission.

And much as she hated to admit it, a lot of what he said made sense. She did still harbor a deep-seated anger. It had bubbled to the surface with surprising force after Scott's first phone call, setting her on edge and bringing back memories of the pain and betrayal she had felt following the accident. It had also brought back her own guilt feelings. And her long-suppressed "what if" questions.

Mark was right about one thing, she acknowledged. There were unresolved issues in her life. Yet something held her back from talking with Scott. Until now, she'd thought it was anger and hatred. But suddenly, with startling clarity, she realized that her reluctance was fueled by something else entirely.

Fear.

And even more troubling, she had no idea why she was afraid.

Chapter Five

Jess turned off the engine and drew a shaky breath. She ought to stop coming here, she told herself as she gazed at the neat rows of headstones that surrounded her. Despite the peaceful, parklike environment, this annual trek always threw her emotions into turmoil. So much so that each year, when she left, she told herself it was her last visit. That she would end this heartbreaking ritual. And each year, when Elizabeth's birthday dawned, she found herself heading back again.

Maybe this time it would be easier, she thought hopefully as she reached for the pink sweetheart rose surrounded by baby's breath and fern. For a moment she gazed at the single, perfect blossom, then gently touched the delicate petals. Pink had been Elizabeth's favorite color, she recalled wistfully, her throat tightening with emotion. And the joyful, optimistic color had suited her. But today, the gray, overcast April sky better reflected her own mood, Jess acknowledged with a sigh.

As she began the trek to the painfully familiar spot where her daughter had been laid to rest, Jess thought back to another bleak, rainy day nearly four years before, when she'd followed this same path in the wake of the small casket carried by her father and brother. The ceremony had been private, just family and a few close friends, as she had requested. Though Scott had been out on bail, she had hoped he would honor her wishes and stay away. But when she arrived at the cemetery he had been there, along with Karen and her family. They stood on one side of the grave, she and her family on the other, the gulf that had separated them far wider than the narrow opening in the ground.

She'd glanced once at Scott—only once—during the brief service. The raw grief in his haggard face, the desperate apology in his eyes had been powerful enough to penetrate her own mantle of sorrow and momentarily touch her heart. But she'd quickly averted her gaze, refusing to be moved by his anguish. He deserved to suffer for what he had done, she'd thought, hatred welling up inside her. And she never wanted to see him again. At her lawyer's request, he had cleared his things out of their house while she was in the hospital recovering from the concussion she had sustained in the accident. By the time she returned home, there was little evidence that he'd ever lived there. She had no idea where he'd gone. And she didn't care.

When the minister finished his prayers, he'd walked over and offered words of condolence that echoed hollowly in her heart. She'd listened numbly until he'd said that the Lord would watch over her in her sorrow, and then anger had bubbled up inside her. It had taken every ounce of her willpower not to lash out at him, to ask where the Lord had been the night Elizabeth had died in a wreckage of twisted metal while Scott had walked away untouched. As if sensing her feelings, her parents had pressed close beside her, thanking the minister in her place. Then they had gently taken her arms, urging her to leave.

As she'd stumbled unseeingly across the grassy expanse, her eyes blinded by tears, she had taken one final glance over her shoulder. Karen and her family had moved off to one side, leaving Scott alone beside the small casket. He was crouched down, one hand resting on the smooth surface. As if sensing her gaze, he had looked up at her, his eyes bleak and lost and almost shell-shocked, as if to say, "How did this happen? How can Elizabeth be gone? And how have we come to this, you and I, we who were once so happy and so in love?"

But Jess had simply turned away, leaving him alone with questions to which she had no answers.

Jess choked back a sob as she now retraced her steps on this familiar path, digging in the pocket of her raincoat for a tissue. She still had no answers, nearly four years later. All she knew was that she wished she could go back to the time of Elizabeth's birth, before the seductive glamour of success had eaten away at the foundation of their marriage, when their three-person circle of love had been the center of their world. That had been the happiest time in her life.

Her eyes filled with tears, and she dabbed at the corners with her tissue, trying to clear her vision so that she didn't trip on the uneven turf or a ground-level headstone. In fact, she was so focused on her footing that she had almost reached Elizabeth's grave before she realized that someone was already there.

Jess stopped abruptly and stared at the familiar broad back. It was Scott, on his knees, sitting back on his heels, a discarded flowerpot and trowel beside him. One of his hands rested on the small headstone, and his head was bent.

Jess almost stopped breathing. She did *not* want to see Scott again! Especially here. For a moment panic overwhelmed her, but she forced herself to think logically. Her best plan was to make a quiet retreat, drive around for a few minutes, then return after he'd gone, she decided. Her heart hammering in her chest, she turned and began to walk rapidly away. But she'd gone only a few steps when his voice reached out to her across the stillness.

"Jess."

The intensity in his hoarse plea made her step falter.

"Please. Stay."

She wanted to ignore him. Wanted to keep walking. But something in his voice reached deep into her soul, compelling her to turn. And once she did, there was no way she could walk away.

Scott was still on his knees, his face raw with grief. Tears ran unchecked down his face, and the anguish in his eyes so closely mirrored what was in her heart that she could almost feel his pain as hers. At least in this one thing they still shared a tragic bond, she realized, her throat tightening with emotion.

They stared at each other in silence for a long moment, their gazes locked, and then Scott slowly rose, never breaking eye contact. Finally, with an effort, he tore his gaze from hers and transferred it to the flower she held.

"I see we both had the same idea," he said softly.

Jess glanced down at the grave to find that he had planted a miniature pink rosebush in front of the headstone. Her eyes blurred with tears, and she took several deep breaths, blinking rapidly to clear her vision. She would *not* break down, she told herself fiercely. She would cry later, in private, as she had been doing for the past four years. She was not going to share her grief with the man who had caused it.

When she finally worked up the courage to gaze at him again, she realized that Scott didn't seem to share her concern about revealing his emotions. With a jolt of surprise she noted that he'd made no attempt to erase the evidence of his tears. She stared at him, completely taken aback by this uncharacteristic behavior. In all the years she'd known him, she'd never seen him cry. He'd been stoic through sadness and through pain, priding himself on his strength to endure all that came his way. Now he stood before her in undisguised grief, seemingly comfortable with his vulnerability. Offering yet more evidence that he had truly changed, she acknowledged reluctantly.

Scott reached down to retrieve the pot and trowel, then stepped aside in silent invitation for Jess to come forward and place her own offering on the grave. For a moment she hesitated. What she really wanted to do was retreat to the safety of her car. She felt off balance, unsure how to react to this new Scott, no clue what he might do next. As if he understood her confusion and uncertainty, he backed off several paces to allow her to maintain a sense of personal space.

Jess realized that turning away at this point would be foolish. So she moved forward slowly until she stood directly in front of the headstone. She rested her hand on the smooth stone, as Scott had done, then knelt and gently laid the rose on the grave. After a moment she raised her gaze to her daughter's name, etched in granite, and with an unsteady hand ran her fingers over the letters. Elizabeth Grace Mitchell. Her gaze lingered on the name she and Scott had so carefully chosen to honor their mothers, a combination of their middle names. Then her gaze moved lower, to the dates of Elizabeth's brief life, and finally to the words at the end. "Cherished daughter of Jess and Scott Mitchell." At first she'd planned to put only her name in the inscription. But in the end, when it had come time to erect the headstone several months after the interment, she'd been unable to leave Scott's name off. For all his sins, she'd never doubted his love for Elizabeth.

"Thank you for that. I didn't expect it."

Scott's voice, raw with emotion, told her that the gesture had not been lost on him.

"I know you loved her, Scott," she whispered brokenly, her head bent as she fought the tears that threatened to spill from her eyes.

Scott's gut clenched painfully as he looked at the woman he loved, kneeling in grief on the grave of the daughter he'd killed, her slender shoulders hunched in anguish. Her hair had swung forward, hiding her face, but he could imagine the emotions that were reflected there. Because they were the same ones that were in his heart. A sense of loss that left you cold and empty inside. A dark despair that made you wonder if life would ever be bright again. A deep, aching loneliness that never went away. And for him there was guilt, as well. Deep, wrenching guilt that had almost driven him mad, until Reverend Young had helped him to believe in, and open himself to, the healing power of God. Though it had taken many months, he had finally made his peace with the Almighty. But in many ways, that had been easier than the challenge he faced with Jess, he realized with a heavy heart. Because God was always willing to give those who repented a second chance. The same didn't necessarily hold true for people. Even for those who have loved us.

Scott yearned to reach down and pull Jess into his arms, to hold her until the remorse and love in his heart seeped into the core of her being, until she knew beyond the shadow of a doubt that he had changed, that his love for her had never diminished and that with all his heart he wanted a second chance to prove to her that this time it would be different. No, he couldn't bring Elizabeth back. Dear God, he would give his life if he could! But he would do everything in his power to bring joy back into Jess's life and to be the husband she deserved, one who never forgot that the greatest of gifts was love.

Once more Jess laid her hand on top of the small monument and then made a move to stand. Instinctively Scott stepped beside her, reaching down to assist her. At his touch on her arm she turned, startled, and he almost backed off at the alarm in her eyes. But something told him to remain where he was.

"Let me help," he said quietly, holding his ground.

She stared at him wide-eyed. Even through her raincoat she could feel the firm, sure touch of his fingers. Her breath caught in her throat as memories came flooding back of the way his strong but gentle hands had always known how to work magic. To be comforting, sensuous, powerful, playful, depending on her mood or her need. He'd been so attuned to her emotions in the beginning that it had sometimes taken her breath away, she recalled with a pang. But that, too, had changed as ambition usurped his energy and attention.

For a long moment they simply looked at each other, their gazes locked, until the overpowering intensity finally compelled Jess into action. With Scott's assistance she rose shakily to her feet, then quickly stepped back, forcing him to drop his hold.

Scott seemed as shaken as she was by the brief touch. She saw his Adam's apple bob convulsively when he swallowed, saw him take a deep breath. Then he withdrew the Bible that had been tucked under his arm.

"Do you mind if I read a verse?" he asked in a voice that was ragged around the edges.

Jess shrugged, and when she replied her own voice was none too steady. "If you want to."

"Is there anything special you'd like to hear?"

"It doesn't matter."

He looked at her curiously. "You always had favorite verses. I'm sorry to say I don't remember what they were. I guess I never paid much attention in those days. But I'd be happy to read one if you'd remind me."

Her gaze cooled. "It really doesn't matter," she said more firmly. "I don't read the Bible anymore."

He frowned. "Why not?"

"I haven't kept up with my faith since…for the last few years."

His eyes filled with understanding and compassion. "It's hard to believe when things happen that don't make sense."

"That doesn't seem to be the case for you."

His eyes grew troubled. "Before I found my way back to the Lord, I had some pretty dark days, Jess," he said quietly.

She thought of Karen's comments about Scott's time in prison. How he had wanted to die. How he lost forty pounds in the first few months. How his hands had shaken so badly. How he'd always had a hopeless look in his eyes. And how she had worried about him every day. Apparently he had truly known some dark—and desperate—days. Which made Scott's return to the Lord even more remarkable, she realized.

"So what happened to renew your faith?" she heard herself asking.

"One of the prison chaplains took me under his wing. Made me realize that I wasn't as alone as I felt, that the Lord doesn't desert us even when we make terrible, tragic mistakes. I didn't buy it at first. But finally, after months of talking and prayer, I began to feel His healing power in my heart.''

"Lucky you." Jess had meant to sound sarcastic. But underlying the sarcasm was an unmistakable wistfulness.

"It wasn't luck. It was a miracle," he said simply.

She had no response to that.

He held up the Bible again. "Do you mind?"

Silently she shook her head.

Scott opened the book and thumbed through it familiarly, stopping when he came to Psalms. And then, in a steady, measured voice he began to read a passage that Jess had once known by heart.

"'The Lord is my shepherd; I shall not want. In verdant pastures He gives me repose; beside restful waters He leads me; He refreshes my soul. He guides me in right paths for His name's sake. Even though I walk in the dark valley I fear no evil; for You are at my side with Your rod and Your staff that give me courage. You spread the table before me in the sight of my foes; You anoint my head with oil; my cup overflows. Only goodness and kindness follow me all the days of my life; and I shall dwell in the house of the Lord for years to come.'"

Scott slowly closed the book, then bowed his head. "Lord, we ask You to keep our Elizabeth in Your care on this, her birthday. We know she is wrapped in Your love, which far surpasses any joy that this world offers. But please help her know that she is loved and remembered by her mother and me, as well. And please give us who are left behind the grace and courage to carry on until the day we are all reunited in Your heavenly kingdom. Amen.''

Jess looked at Scott's bowed head, his fervent prayer echoing in her heart, and suddenly she understood why she'd been afraid to talk with him. Somehow, intuitively, she had known that if she did, the wall of hatred she'd so carefully constructed would begin to crumble. Because she would be forced to admit that at heart he was a good man who had simply made tragic mistakes. Yes, the consequences of his actions had been terrible. But the actions themselves had not been undertaken with any malice. That acknowledgment, coupled with the striking changes in his personality, made it harder and harder to maintain the wall that separated them. And without that wall, she would be vulnerable again. To hurt. To betrayal. To loss. That was why she was afraid.

When Scott raised his head and glanced at Jess, his breath momentarily lodged in his throat. For the briefest second, in her unguarded eyes, he saw something that hadn't been there before. He wouldn't go so far as to call it warmth. But there was a…softer…look in her eyes. It was slight. It was very subtle. But it was there. And it gave him renewed hope.

Suddenly a gentle rain began to fall, and he tucked the Bible protectively in his jacket, then zipped it up. ''I guess it's time to go.''

Jess nodded. She glanced once more at the grave, where the pink flowers provided the only spot of color on this gray day. She hoped somehow that Scott's prayer had been heard, that her daughter would know that she was still deeply loved and sorely missed. "Happy birthday, Elizabeth," she whispered.

When she looked back at Scott, he was standing quietly, watching her. "You were a wonderful mother, Jess," he said hoarsely. "Just like you were a wonderful wife."

The unexpectedness of the comment took her off guard, and she had no idea how to respond. So instead she ignored it, confining her comment to a simple goodbye. Then she turned and walked toward her car.

She didn't look back, though she felt his gaze on her. And once in her car, hidden from his view, she sat for several minutes until her trembling subsided.

When she at last put the car into gear, she circled back toward the entrance, glancing once more at Elizabeth's grave in the distance. To her surprise, Scott was still there, though the rain had intensified. He seemed oblivious to the cold drops of water as he stared down at the grave, a solitary figure in the gray landscape, his hands in the pockets of his denim jacket. And somehow she knew that raindrops weren't the only moisture on his cheeks.

"Oh, Frank, look at this one!"

Jess and her father glanced toward Clare, who was standing in awe over a particularly stunning specimen of iris.

"I think I'll be adding another one to the list," he grumbled good-naturedly, taking a small notebook out of his pocket as they headed toward the older woman.

"Frank, write this one down," she said excitedly when they drew close.

"Sure thing," Frank replied, pausing to give Jess an "I-told-you-so" look. "But honey, where are you going to put all of these? The bed is full already."

"I could say the same about your roses," she countered with an affectionate smile.

"Touché," he acknowledged fondly.

Jess smiled. Her parents' devotion to each other had always been an inspiration to her. Theirs was the kind of marriage she had always hoped to create, where love came first. Though her father had worked hard in a blue-collar job all his life, often coming home tired after a long day, he'd always made it a priority to spend time each evening with his wife and children. He'd rarely missed a school event or a dance recital, and each summer he'd pile the four of them into the family car, attach a pop-up camper that he'd bought secondhand, and they'd head out for a new adventure somewhere in the United States. Her mother had been equally devoted to the family, taking time each day when Jess and Mark arrived home from school to listen to their chatter over a glass of milk and cookies. It had been an idyllic childhood, and Jess would be forever grateful for the support and love her parents had lavished on their children.

Nor would she ever forget their support after Elizabeth's death. Without their intervention, she didn't know if she would have survived the dark days that followed. She'd lost a daughter, a husband and a whole way of life in the space of a few hours. For all intents and purposes, her world had come to an end. She, too, had walked through the valley of darkness mentioned in the Bible verse Scott had read at the cemetery . But unlike him, she had found no comfort in her faith. She owed her salvation to the love and support of her family.

"What do you think, Jess?"

With a start, Jess came back to reality. Her parents were looking at her questioningly, but she had no idea what they'd asked. "Sorry. I was daydreaming. What did you say?"

Her father nodded to two different irises. "Which one do you like better?"

She moved forward and studied the two delicate, frilly blossoms, one in shades of purple, the other white with a purple edge. "That one," she said decisively, pointing to the latter.

Her mother looked pleased. "I agree. Write that one down, Frank. I think I'll put that one in the…" Her mother's voice trailed off, and her eyes grew wide as she stared over Jess's shoulder.

Before Jess could turn to discover the source of her mother's distraction, a familiar voice spoke.

"Hello, Clare, Frank. Hello, Jess."

Jess's gaze moved from her mother's shocked face to her father's cold, contemptuous expression, then slowly she turned. Scott was standing just a few feet behind her, dressed in jeans and a long-sleeved shirt worn the way he'd always preferred, with the sleeves slightly rolled up. He was carrying what looked like a sketch pad, and his dark brown eyes gazed at her warmly.

"What are you doing here?" Jess asked, realizing even as she spoke that this was becoming her common greeting to Scott.

A smile tugged at the corners of his mouth, as if he had had the same thought. "The same thing you are, I expect. Enjoying a beautiful day at the garden. I often come on Saturday morning."

"Jess, isn't it time to leave for the brunch?"

At her father's terse question, she turned back to him. He was pointedly ignoring Scott, and she could see the anger smoldering in his eyes. It was far too soon to leave for the restaurant, but clearly Scott's appearance had ruined the garden for her parents.

"We should be okay, Dad," she replied, struggling to maintain an even, pleasant tone.

At her response, his mouth thinned. "I think we should go," he repeated more forcefully. "Your mother and I have seen enough here." He glanced pointedly at Scott, then turned away.

Jess knew how much her parents despised Scott for what he had done, but she was nevertheless taken aback by her father's uncharacteristic display of ill manners. She turned, an apology in her eyes, to find that a hot flush of embarrassment had crept up Scott's neck.

"I need to move on, too," he said quietly. "I'm heading for the Japanese garden. That's probably where I'll spend the next couple of hours." He was letting them know where he'd be so they could avoid him, Jess realized, struck by his thoughtfulness despite her father's rudeness. "It was good to see you again, Jess. Frank, Clare, enjoy the rest of your day."

With that he turned and walked away.

Scott was barely out of earshot when Frank spoke.

"Good riddance!" he said vehemently.

"Dad!"

"What?"

"He might hear you."

"So what if he does? I want him to know exactly what I think of him."

"He looks older," Clare said thoughtfully.

"He *is* older," Frank replied curtly.

"I just mean that prison must have been hard on him."

"Good."

Jess stuck her hands into the pockets of her slacks. "Don't you think you're being a little harsh, Dad?"

He looked at her stiffly. "Not particularly. He killed my granddaughter. And practically ruined my daughter's life. He deserves whatever suffering has come his way. I thought you felt the same way."

"I do," she replied, but her voice lacked conviction.

Clare gave Jess a troubled look. "Honey, has something happened? Is there something you haven't told us?"

Actually, there was. She'd never mentioned her unexpected meetings with Scott—at the hospital, her condo, the cemetery. Nor the unsettling effect they'd had on her. She needed to work through her feelings on her own, unbiased by the strong negative feelings her parents had about Scott.

She shrugged. "He seems different, that's all."

"Well, I expect he is, after three years in prison," Clare concurred.

"That doesn't absolve him from what he did," Frank maintained stubbornly. "Or change the consequences."

"No, of course not," Clare agreed.

Frank moved beside Jess and laid a hand on her shoulder. "Honey, you know we just want what's best for you," he said, gentling his voice. "And Scott isn't it. Maybe he's changed. I don't know. Frankly, I don't *want* to know. Because it doesn't matter. He's no longer a part of our life. I'm sorry we ran into him today, but he's really just a stranger to us now. He can't do anything more to hurt us. And as long as we keep shutting him out we're safe. Right?"

"Right," Jess responded automatically.

But in her heart Jess didn't feel safe at all.

Jess propped the bag of groceries on her hip as she retrieved her mail, then tucked it under her arm as she fitted her key in the lock. Once inside, she deposited the bag on the counter and quickly flipped through mostly ads and junk, shaking her head sympathetically for the overburdened mail carriers.

At the bottom of the stack was a flyer from her former church, and she gazed at it with a frown. She had no idea why she was still on the mailing list. She hadn't been an active member of the congregation for almost four years. She ought to just call and tell them to remove her name, she thought, glancing uninterestedly at the information about an upcoming retreat. She was just about to toss it into the trash with all the other junk mail when the last name listed under "speakers" caught her eye. Scott Mitchell.

With a frown, she glanced again at the theme of the event. "Coping with Adversity: Ask and You Shall Receive." It went on to say that a number of clergy would discuss the topic theologically, and that various individuals with extraordinary stories would talk about their personal faith experiences.

Slowly Jess sat down at the kitchen table, the groceries forgotten for the moment. Scott had shared a great deal with her during their marriage, but she couldn't recall a single incident when he'd opened up to other people. Especially about painful experiences or disappointments. How in the world had they talked him into this? she wondered incredulously.

Even more intriguing was the content of his talk. He'd said virtually nothing to her about his experiences in prison, referring only to "some pretty dark days." But what had actually happened? How dark was "dark"? And how had he found his way through the maze of despair back to faith?

Of course, there was no way she was going to attend this event, Jess told herself impatiently as she tossed the brochure onto the counter and turned her attention to the perishable items in her grocery bag. She wasn't *that* curious. And frankly, she didn't really *want* to know what had happened to Scott during his years behind bars. Partly because she felt he deserved whatever had occurred. But mostly because she was afraid that if she found out, the wall between them would crumble even more.

Chapter Six

"Excuse me...do you work here?"

Scott turned to find an older couple standing behind him. "Yes. Can I help you?" he asked pleasantly.

The man nodded toward the display of balled and burlapped dogwood trees in the nursery lot. "I'd like to get one of those for my yard, but I don't know much about trees. I need some advice."

Scott glanced around, but none of the retail staff was in the area. "I usually work on the commercial side of the business," he said hesitantly, unwilling to overstep the clear bounds Seth had set for his job. On the other hand, he doubted the owner would consider it good customer relations to leave this couple while he went in search of a salesperson. Especially when he could very likely help them. "I'll tell you what. Why don't you ask me your questions, and if I can't answer them I'll find someone who can."

"Fair enough," agreed the man. "My wife and I

have always liked dogwood trees, but we hear they're a bit temperamental. Any truth to that?''

''Well, they are subject to a few more problems than some trees,'' Scott verified, setting his shovel aside. ''But a lot of ornamentals are like that. You'd need to watch for borers, which can eat away under the bark and eventually kill the tree. But it's easy to spot the signs, and the problem is relatively simple to treat. So I wouldn't let that stop you if you have your heart set on a dogwood. And they *are* a native Missouri tree, so they tend to do well here. What kind of sun exposure will it have?''

''We want to put it on the east side of the house. Lots of sun in the morning, but it's pretty shaded there in the afternoon.''

Scott nodded. ''That's good. Dogwoods don't handle full sun very well. They're also relatively slow growers. So while they have a spreading aspect, it will take a long time before you have much of a display, even with a fairly large tree. And it can sometimes take a year or two before they bloom.''

''Hmm. Time isn't on our side, is it, Rose?'' the man said, smiling affectionately at the older woman. ''We aren't exactly spring chickens.''

''If I could suggest something, then...''

''Certainly.''

''You might want to plant a *grouping* of dogwoods. Maybe mix the pink and white. If you have a large enough area, that could work very nicely. And you'd have a lot more color a lot sooner.''

''Well now, I hadn't thought about that. A grove.''

The man considered that for a moment, then turned to his wife. "What do you think, Rose?"

"It sounds lovely."

"Is there any other landscaping in the area?" Scott asked as an idea began to take shape in his mind.

"No. We never did much on the side yard. But we just added a conservatory to the house, and now we have a great view of that part of our property."

"In that case, depending on your budget, of course, you might want to do a mulch bed that links the trees together. Maybe put in a few azaleas and some shade-loving perennials like hostas."

"This is sounding better and better," the man said enthusiastically. "Do you think you could come out to the house, take a look at the area, show us some ideas?"

Now Scott *knew* he'd overstepped his bounds. He was a laborer, not a landscape consultant—even if that *was* his long-term goal. But breaking the rules wasn't likely to move him in that direction. "Actually, I don't usually..."

"He'll be glad to."

Scott turned sharply at the sound of Seth's voice, and hot color stole up his neck. The owner stood only a few feet away and had apparently overheard the entire exchange.

"That would be great," the older man said.

"Why don't we go inside and take a look at the appointment book and we'll set something up," Seth told the man. Then he turned to Scott. "See me when you finish up here."

Scott nodded, a sick feeling in the pit of his stomach. Seth had made the ground rules very clear when he started. Stick to your job. Ask for help when you need it. And don't confuse the two parts of the business—commercial and retail. Scott had clearly violated that rule. Which could not only derail his hopes of eventually moving into landscape design, but cost him his job. Reverend Young had warned him that Seth was a hard taskmaster who didn't tolerate insubordination. And that's exactly the way he might interpret Scott's action, though it certainly hadn't been the intent.

Scott finished shoveling the pile of mulch as quickly as possible, then headed for Seth's office, praying that the owner would at least listen to his explanation. Seth was on the phone when Scott arrived, and he motioned the younger man to take a seat.

"Look, Mike, we agreed on a Wednesday delivery, and that's when I need it," Seth said in a clipped tone. "I've got a commercial job starting on Thursday, and those boxwoods are a major part of it. What am I supposed to tell my customer? And who's going to pay the crew to stand around all day?" Seth chomped on his unlit cigar for a moment as he listened, his expression implacable. "Yeah. Yeah. Okay," he finally said. "Get me fifty of them Wednesday. I can hold off on the rest till Thursday. But no later. You got that?"

Seth dropped the receiver back into the cradle and turned his penetrating gaze on Scott. "So you want to tell me what that was all about?"

Scott took a deep breath. "I'm sorry if I overstepped. There wasn't anyone around to help those customers, so I thought it would be better if I—''

''Whoa!'' Seth held up his hand, then leaned forward, propping his elbows on the desk. ''That's not what I meant. Where did you learn so much about trees?''

Scott stared at his boss, taken aback. Apparently he wasn't angry after all. Relief flooded through him and he slowly let out the breath he hadn't even realized he was holding. ''I've always enjoyed horticulture. And landscaping. I read a lot about it in prison, and I worked on the vegetable gardens and helped with the groundskeeping while I was there.''

''You ever do any landscape design?''

''Not officially. But I've studied that, too, and I've done quite a few sketches.''

''You still have them?''

''Yes.''

''Bring them in tomorrow.''

''I also designed and installed a meditation garden at Reverend Young's church,'' Scott offered.

Seth looked at him appraisingly. ''When did you do that?''

''On Saturdays.''

''Don't you do enough digging during the week?''

Scott shrugged. ''I owe a lot to Reverend Young. I didn't mind.''

Seth studied him for a moment longer, then consulted the work schedule. ''Plan on going over to Mr. Hudson's house on Friday.''

''I'm supposed to be on the crew over at the hospital then,'' Scott reminded him.

The older man waved the objection aside. "Laborers I can always find. Though not always as dependable as you," he added, giving Scott his first real—if backhanded—compliment. "People who know plants and have an eye for design are a lot tougher to find. So bring in those drawings. And I'll swing by that meditation garden on my way home." Seth reached for the phone, signaling the end of the discussion.

But as Scott rose and headed for the door, Seth stopped him with one final comment.

"You show promise," he said gruffly. "Keep this up, and things should work out just fine for you here."

A smile flashed across Scott's face. "Thanks."

As he left the office, Scott's heart felt lighter than it had in a long while. Somehow, earning Seth's respect meant more to him than all the bonuses he'd received in his former job. Because those were impersonal, determined by a formula that was revenue based. Seth's compliments, on the other hand—and his encouragement—seemed much more personal. And therefore more meaningful.

And best of all, if things went well with the Hudsons, maybe that project would open the door for Scott to begin building a new career.

Jess closed the folder, slid it back into her file drawer and glanced at her watch. She'd been in her office only twenty minutes, hardly long enough to justify a special trip into town on Saturday. Especially since she didn't have to give the presentation until the middle of next week.

Admit it, she told herself with a sigh. There was no

legitimate business reason for this trip. Her *real* motives were purely personal, and to pretend otherwise was foolish. Since meeting Scott in the garden the week before, she'd been unable to forget his comment that he often came here on Saturdays. And deep in her heart, she wanted to see him again. Even though it made no sense.

She rose and restlessly walked over to the window, staring down unseeingly at the manicured grounds. For the past three months she'd gone out of her way to avoid him and, on the occasions when their paths *had* crossed, to make it clear that she wanted nothing to do with him. Yet now she was deliberately putting herself in a position to meet him. Which was probably a big mistake.

Her parents would certainly think so, she acknowledged. They considered any contact with Scott to be bad news. That was why she'd never told them about the times she'd run into him. Or about her plans for today. What would she say? That she was intrigued by the changes in him, driven by some powerful force deep inside to learn more about the transformation that had occurred during his time in prison? They would hardly be receptive to that message. Nor would they understand her change in attitude. And frankly, neither did she.

Jess sighed again. If she was smart, she would probably just turn around and go home. But she hadn't been feeling especially smart lately. Just unsettled. And going home was unlikely to change that. So she might as well follow her instincts.

Resignedly she reached for her purse, flipped off the

lights in her office and headed out into the garden. The cobalt-blue sky of early morning had given way to scattered clouds, but she took little notice of the weather—or the beauty around her. She was looking for only one thing—a tall, broad-shouldered man with a glint of silver in his dark hair. Nothing else registered in her field of vision.

Thirty minutes later, however, after a rapid but complete circuit of the grounds, she'd seen no sign of Scott. Which was probably good, she assured herself even as a feeling of disappointment swept over her. Trying to engineer a chance meeting had been silly. And not very smart.

She hitched her shoulder purse higher and resolutely headed toward the exit, rebuking herself for wasting so much of her day on a whim. She could have spent a lazy morning catching up on some reading, paying bills or doing something far more productive than...

"Jess!"

At the sound of the familiar voice, her heart ratcheted into triple time and she froze. So he was here after all. She forced herself to take a deep, calming breath, then slowly turned. He was striding toward her, dressed in exactly the same manner as last week, the same notebook under his arm, his expression surprised—and delighted.

"I thought it was you." His eyes smiled warmly into hers before he broke contact to glance cautiously around. "Are you alone?"

She nodded, struggling to find her voice. "Yes."

His smile broadened. "Good."

She couldn't blame him for his reaction, not after

their last encounter in the gardens. "Listen…about last week…my father…"

He smiled gently. "It's okay, Jess. I understand how he feels about me. He has a right."

Does he? she suddenly wondered as she stared into Scott's kind eyes. *Was* it right to hate in the face of true remorse and regret? At some point didn't hate become more destructive to the hater than the person hated? Wasn't forgiveness a part of healing, as her brother had inferred? But she voiced none of those troubling questions, tucking them away in her mind for later consideration. "Well, it was rude nonetheless."

"I'm used to a lot worse."

The words were said matter-of-factly, but she saw the flash of pain in his eyes. Clearly, the horrors of prison life had left an indelible mark, though he didn't dwell on the subject.

"Now I'm going to steal your question," he continued with an engaging grin. "What are you doing here?"

"I, uh, had to stop at my office. To go over a presentation."

He gave her a puzzled look. "So how did you end up here?"

"I work here."

He looked surprised. "At the garden?"

"Yes. In public relations."

"No kidding! That's great!"

"I like it." She knew her responses sounded stilted, but she couldn't help it. That's how she felt. Stiff. And awkward. And uncomfortable. Especially knowing that she had engineered this "chance" meeting.

"So are you leaving now?"

She nodded. "I just stopped in for a few minutes."

"Can I buy you a cup of coffee first? The outdoor café would be great on a day like this."

Jess stared at him. A casual meeting, a few words exchanged in passing were one thing. Spending time with him seemed somehow...wrong. As if by doing so she would somehow dishonor the memory of Elizabeth and be disloyal to her parents. At the same time, she thought about Mark's advice. He had encouraged her to talk with Scott, suggested that the only way to truly let go of the past was to face it. And more and more lately, she had begun to admit that he might be right.

Scott waited patiently for Jess's response, struggling to maintain a placid expression even though his heart was hammering painfully in his chest. He knew he was pushing things with his invitation, but what did he have to lose? At worst, she would say no. At best...well, that remained to be seen. But even a few minutes in her company, in this neutral setting of natural beauty, was bound to do *some* good. It *had* to. He'd prayed for guidance, for opportunity and for the right words when the time came. The Lord had certainly provided the first two. Now Scott hoped that He would come through on the last, as well.

As Scott waited for Jess to reply he used the moment to simply drink in the sight of her. For three long years he had had nothing but dreams to sustain him. Dreams of her kindness, her beauty, her joy. Of the way her eyes had once shone with love when they gazed at him. Of his hope of winning her heart all over again. Those were the dreams he had clung to.

And now Jess stood only a whisper away, no longer a dream but flesh and blood. She was close, so close. And yet so far. Reachable but not touchable, though the urge to do so grew stronger with each encounter. But until he saw welcome and warmth in her eyes, rather than the caution and conflict now reflected in them as she pondered his invitation, he knew that patience—and prudence—were his friends. Whether he liked it or not.

As the seconds ticked by, Jess realized she had to make a decision. But for some reason her brain didn't seem to be functioning. Her *heart,* on the other hand, had kicked into overdrive, urging her to follow her brother's advice and talk with Scott. And as she gazed into his warm brown eyes, her doubts somehow melted away. After all, it was only a cup of coffee. What harm could it do? In fact, if her brother was right, some *good* might come of it.

With sudden decision, she nodded. "All right. I have time for a quick cup."

If it wouldn't have attracted so much attention, Scott would have fallen to his knees on the spot. As it was, he simply sent a silent, heartfelt thank-you heavenward. "Great! Why don't you pick out a table and I'll get the coffee?" he suggested, struggling to contain the elation in his voice.

"Okay. Just a little cream."

He smiled then, that lazy, smoky smile that had always turned her knees to rubber. "I remember," he said softly. Their gazes connected for a brief second before he turned away, but it was long enough for her to see the heat simmering in the depths of his eyes. "I'll meet you on the terrace," he said over his shoulder.

Jess stared after him, caught off guard by the intimate, husky timbre of his voice and the look in his eyes, which had opened a floodgate of memories. She had never been a morning person, and when they were first married Scott had gotten into the habit of rising first to make coffee. Then he'd bring her a cup in bed, slipping in beside her to sip his as she slowly woke up. And sometimes, especially in the cold days of winter when neither wanted to leave their warm cocoon, they'd snuggle back under the covers for a few stolen moments. So yes, Scott knew exactly how she liked her coffee. And other things, as well.

A surge of longing suddenly swept over Jess, so strong and so unexpected that she gasped, causing a passerby to pause and gaze at her in alarm.

"Are you all right, dear?" the older woman asked in concern.

Jess felt her face grow red, and she nodded jerkily. "Yes. I—I'm fine."

The woman didn't appear to be convinced. "Are you sure? Would you like to sit down?"

"No, really, I'm fine."

An older man came up beside the woman and glanced curiously at Jess. "What's wrong, Ellen?"

"I thought perhaps this young woman was ill."

By now they were drawing inquisitive glances from

those seated nearby, and Jess felt her color deepen. "I appreciate your concern, but…"

"Is something wrong?"

Jess turned to find Scott gazing at her with a troubled look, but before she could speak the older woman chimed in.

"Oh, are you with this young man, dear? Well, Harry, she's in good hands. I'm sure he'll see to her if she isn't well. You take care, miss," she said over her shoulder as they headed toward an empty table.

Jess closed her eyes, wanting to drop through the floor in embarrassment. How in the world was she going to explain that exchange to Scott? she wondered desperately. There was no way on earth she could tell him the truth!

"Jess?"

She forced herself to open her eyes and meet Scott's gaze. He looked even more concerned now, and a slight frown marred his brow. "What was that all about? Are you sick?"

Jess swallowed. "No. I'm fine. Where would you like to sit?"

Scott ignored her question, titling his head to study her face. "You look a little flushed."

But not because I'm sick! she thought silently, glad that he couldn't read her mind. "I'm fine, really," she repeated more firmly. "How about that table over by the railing? We can see the roses from there."

He hesitated for a moment, then much to her relief let the subject drop. In fact, he seemed a little distracted himself—which was okay with her. "That's fine," he agreed.

Scott followed her to the small café table, still berating himself for his response to her comment about the coffee. He'd have to be more guarded in the future. He needed to avoid topics that would make him recall the intimate details of their marriage. Because a few more slips like that and he could easily scare her off.

"The roses are great this year, aren't they? Does your father still have his rose garden?" he asked with studied casualness as he deposited the cups and his notebook on the table.

She nodded. "Bigger than ever. It's become almost an obsession since he retired two years ago. He's got a couple of bushes right now that he's hovering over like a mother hen, in preparation for a show in July. So much so that he threatened not to go with us on vacation next week."

"A family vacation?"

"Yes. To Padre Island."

"Sounds nice."

"We've been going there the last few years. Mom and Dad really like it." But she didn't want to talk about her parents. Knowing how they felt about Scott, she could imagine their reaction to this little tête-à-tête. So she changed the subject, pointing to his notebook. "What's that for?"

"Landscaping ideas. I've done a lot of reading about the subject in the last few years, and I've dabbled in design. The botanical garden always inspires me, so I try to drop by on Saturday mornings whenever I can."

She looked at him curiously. "I thought you'd lost interest in that sort of thing years ago."

"Not really. I just didn't have the time to devote to it. However, time hasn't been a problem these past few years."

The final comment was made lightly, but Jess suspected that for a man like Scott, who had always filled every minute of his day with activity, time must have hung very heavily on his hands in prison. However, that was ground she didn't want to tread on. "So what are you working on now?" she asked.

He hesitated, then reached for the notebook and flipped through a number of detailed drawings, stopping at one that was only partially finished. He handed it to her.

"That one's actually going to see the light of day," he said. "My boss has asked me to work with one of our customers to design this garden."

Jess glanced at him in surprise. There was an undercurrent of pride and excitement in his voice, a boyish enthusiasm, that she hadn't heard in many, many years. As if he truly loved what he was doing.

With interest she studied the detailed layout, drawn precisely on graph paper. It was a woodland cluster of plantings, with several dogwood trees as anchors. The design was pleasant to the eye and very natural looking, though the plotting of the plants and the groupings of perennials had clearly been carefully thought through.

"Very nice. May I?" she asked, nodding toward the notebook.

"Yes. But the designs are pretty rough. This kind of work is mostly done by computer these days, but I...well, I used what I had."

Jess looked again at the meticulous workmanship and shook her head. "I wouldn't exactly call these rough," she disagreed. Each one had clearly been done with great care, and all were appealing. But the one she lingered over longest was a lakeside garden featuring a gazebo. There was something about it, some quality of tranquillity, that touched her soul. "This is lovely," she said softly.

Scott leaned over to see which drawing had caught Jess's eye. "As a matter of fact, that's the only design in the book that has actually been produced," he said, pleased she had singled it out. "It's for a meditation garden at my church."

Jess looked over at him. "You mean this garden really exists?"

"Yes."

She glanced down again, impressed by his talent, touched by a beauty that the black-and-white pencil drawing could only hint at. "I think you may have found your true calling, Scott," she said as she closed the notebook and handed it back to him.

"I think you may be right," he concurred with a satisfied nod. Then he set the notebook aside and smiled at her. "So now tell me about you. How did you end up here?"

She took a sip of her coffee and shrugged. "After...the accident I needed something to do. I volunteered here for a few months, and when the job became available, they offered it to me. It was a perfect fit with my public relations background, and they already knew me from volunteering. I've been here for almost two years."

"Do you like it?"

"Very much. It's pleasant work in a beautiful setting. And it keeps me busy, which is good. Also, since I sold the house I haven't had much opportunity to garden, and being in a place like this helps make up for that."

"Knowing how much you enjoyed working with flowers, I was a little surprised to find you'd moved to a condo," he admitted.

She took a sip of her coffee, gazing at him over the rim of her cup as she tried to discern whether he was upset that she'd sold the "trophy" house he'd once taken such great pride in. But he didn't appear to be disturbed. Just curious. She set the cup on the table and shrugged. "The house was too big just for me. Besides, I didn't feel capable of tackling the upkeep single-handedly. But I do miss having a yard, so I may get another house at some point. I don't know. I just sort of take it a day at a time for now."

He studied her silently for a moment, then sighed and glanced down at his coffee. "I can relate to that. Sometimes that's the only way to survive." When he looked at her again, his eyes were troubled. "Your parents watched out for you after the accident, didn't they?"

Though his tone was quiet, the intensity in his eyes told her clearly that this worry had been on his mind for a long time. She swallowed with difficulty, touched by the depth of his concern in a way she couldn't articulate, then averted her head and looked toward the rose garden. Dear God, yes, she had been alone—and lonely—despite her parents' best efforts to fill the gaps, she recalled, her throat tightening with emotion.

Nevertheless, their love had made a huge difference. In fact, it was only because of them that she had survived.

She drew an unsteady breath, fighting for control, but when she spoke there was a catch in her voice. "They saved my life," she said simply, without looking back at him.

As Scott gazed at her stoic profile, his gut clenched painfully. Night after night in prison he'd lain awake staring into the darkness, praying that God would watch over her and keep her safe, that He would ease her pain. Jess had always been a strong woman. But when he'd seen her at the funeral, he'd known she was balancing precariously on the edge of an emotional breakdown. That only the support of her family, and God's grace, would keep her from falling into the abyss of despair and depression that had already sucked him in.

Clearly, she'd survived and gone on with her life, though it was equally clear that she'd been through hell in the interim. And the ordeal had obviously taken a lasting toll on her, he realized, noting the way her slender fingers were gripping the paper cup, so tightly that the shape was distorted. He longed to reach over and take her hand in a comforting clasp, to promise her that she'd never have to face such trauma alone again. But it was too soon. He knew that intuitively. He had to keep his distance. Physically, at least. But maybe he could put out some feelers on the emotional front.

"How are you *now*, Jess?" he asked gently.

She didn't turn back to him immediately. And when she did, she met his gaze directly with eyes that were dry—and slightly defiant. "I'm fine, Scott," she said as steadily, as convincingly, as she could. She forced herself to hold his gaze for a long moment, hoping he would buy her response—even though she herself was beginning to realize that it was a lie.

Scott didn't dispute her claim. But he didn't believe it, either. She was too fragile emotionally. Too thin physically. And too lost spiritually. She needed him as much as he needed her. But convincing her of that would take time. And he'd gone about as far as was prudent today. Reluctantly he took the last swallow of his coffee and reached for his notebook. "I'm glad things are going well for you, Jess. And it was good to see you today."

She looked at him in surprise, taken aback. He'd seemed so anxious to see her, to talk with her. So why was he was cutting their exchange short? But on the heels of that question came another, more disturbing one. Why should she care? And the answer was clear. She shouldn't. The fact that she *did* only made her angry. Letting Scott back into her life would just set her up for disappointments, she reminded herself. And she'd had enough of those. Abruptly she reached for her purse and stood.

"Thanks for the coffee," she said shortly.

If Scott noticed her change in tone, he gave no indication of it. "My pleasure," he replied, rising in a more leisurely way. "Can I walk you to your car?"

"It's not far."

"I don't mind."

She shrugged. It wasn't worth arguing about. "If you like."

They made their way silently through the main exhibit building, and by the time they exited a light rain had begun to fall. She glanced at the sky with a frown, pausing under the overhang from the building. "You'll get wet if you walk me to my car," she said. "Why don't we just say goodbye here?"

"I'll get wet either way. It doesn't matter," he replied as he withdrew a plastic bag from his pocket and slipped his sketchbook inside.

"But if we each make a dash for our cars we'll only get slightly damp," she persisted.

"I took the bus here, Jess," he said matter-of-factly. "So where are you parked?"

She stared at him. Scott had taken a *bus*? He'd never taken a bus in his life—except maybe in college. Certainly not since she'd known him. Why in the world would he be doing so now?

"You took a bus?" she repeated in confusion.

"Yes."

"Why?"

"I don't have a car yet."

"Why not?"

He gave her a crooked grin. "Because car dealers don't sell cars based on good looks. Although I'm not sure that would necessarily help me even if they did."

Again she stared at him. Frankly, she had never even thought about Scott's financial situation. Of course, she knew he'd signed over his interest in all their assets to her after the trial. Not that she'd asked him to. Or cared one way or the other. At the time finances were the last thing on her mind. She'd simply told her attorney to deal with it and asked no questions. For the first six months she'd simply drawn on her accounts for day-to-day living expenses and counseling. And by the time she was able to take more control over her finances, she simply started from where she was. Her attorney was a trusted family friend with an impeccable reputation, and she'd never doubted his diligent management of her assets. But all along Jess had just assumed that Scott had kept *something* in reserve for himself. A cash account somewhere. Had she been wrong?

"I don't understand," she said, still confused. "Don't you have any money?"

He gave her an easy smile. "Sure. I have a decent job. Seth pays a good wage."

"No, I mean from before."

Now his face grew serious. "Didn't your attorney tell you? I turned everything over to you."

"I knew about the major assets, of course, but I...I guess I just assumed you kept something in reserve for...for when you got out," she replied, growing more and more flustered.

He shook his head. "I wanted you to have everything."

"But that isn't really fair. I mean, I have way more than I need."

"It's fair, Jess. Trust me." His gaze locked with hers, and she knew that this was one subject that was not open to discussion. "So do you want to make a run for it?"

She looked at the rain, which had intensified even as they spoke. Scott would be drenched in a matter of minutes if he had to wait for a bus.

"Why don't you let me drive you home?" she said impulsively.

Scott looked as surprised by the offer as she felt.

"Are you sure?" he said cautiously.

No, she wasn't. In fact, she wasn't sure about a lot of things lately. But ignoring the issues wasn't going to make them go away. Just as avoiding Scott wasn't going to help her resolve her feelings about him.

"Honestly? No. It just...came out," she replied truthfully.

A shadow of disappointment briefly passed over his eyes, but he recovered quickly. "It's okay. I have to make a quick stop on the way home, anyway. It's better if I just take the bus. But thank you. Now, where's your car? I'll still walk with you that far."

She nodded to the right, and he fell in beside her as they rapidly crossed the asphalt. By the time they reached the door she had her key in hand, and she quickly fitted it into the lock and slid inside. She looked up at him to say goodbye, but the words died in her throat as she noted the rain already soaking through his cotton shirt, the lines of weariness in his face, the kindness in his eyes. And when she finally opened her mouth, entirely different words came out.

"I don't mind making a stop, Scott. Get in before you're soaked."

This time he didn't question her motives. After only the slightest hesitation, he simply closed her door and made his way around to the passenger side.

And as she reached over to unlock the door for him, Jess couldn't help but feel that she was opening the door to far more than her car.

Chapter Seven

Scott's physical presence somehow seemed magnified in the confines of Jess's compact car, and she nervously tucked her hair behind her ear before backing out of the parking spot. Somehow sharing her car with him seemed to move their relationship to a new, more personal level.

The significance of the moment wasn't lost on Scott, either. In the three and a half months since his release, his encounters with Jess had always been in public places where other people could see what they were doing and hear what they were saying. By contrast, the intimacy of her car gave them a degree of privacy they hadn't had in almost four years, providing an opportunity to talk about things best discussed behind closed doors. Considering her almost palpable tension, Jess was keenly aware of that, he surmised. She was probably having not just *second* thoughts about her offer of a ride, but third and fourth thoughts. So he needed to put her at ease, assure her he wasn't going to use the situation to introduce topics with which she was not yet comfortable.

"Nice car," he said, deliberately adopting an even, conversational tone. "And it sure beats the bus. Thanks again for the lift."

"No problem." Her voice sounded strained, and she lapsed into silence until they reached the parking-lot exit. "Which way?"

"Left. Then left again at the first light. There's a grocery store a few blocks down. That's where I need to stop."

She turned to him in surprise. "You're going grocery shopping?"

He smiled. "No. I just need to pick up a couple of things for someone."

As they drove the short distance, Scott purposely kept the conversation light. And by the time they pulled into the lot a few minutes later, she seemed to have relaxed slightly.

"Do you want to come in?" he asked.

She shook her head. "I'll wait."

"Okay. I'll only be a few minutes." He stepped out of the car, then leaned back down. "But lock the doors. This isn't the best part of town."

"I work down here, remember?" she reminded him wryly.

"I'll bet you never wander more than a block or two from the garden."

She conceded the point with a nod. "True."

"Good. Keep it that way, okay?" When her eyes widened in surprise, he grinned sheepishly. "Sorry.

Some old habits die hard, I guess. I'll be right back.''
He locked the door before pushing it closed.

Jess watched him until he disappeared inside the
building, then slowly exhaled. She needed a few minute to decompress, to figure out what had happened
back in the parking lot at the botanical garden. Because she'd certainly had no intention of offering Scott
a ride. Not even *once,* let alone *twice.* Yet she hadn't
taken him up on the out he'd offered. Why? There
was no logical explanation for her behavior—except
maybe that she was off balance because of all the
strange things that had happened today, she reasoned,
ticking them off in her mind.

First, Scott's invitation to stop at the café had come
out of the blue. Given her reservations about merely
exchanging a few words in passing, her acceptance
made no sense.

Second, the unexpected eruption of intense longing
in response to his comment about coffee had left her
reeling. Despite the other problems in their marriage,
the attraction between them had never diminished, she
recalled, her mouth suddenly going dry. At least in
that one respect, their marriage had been solid. But
how could he still produce that kind of effect in her
with just one intimate look and two simple words,
when she'd spent the past four years hating him? That
made even less sense.

Third, his abrupt ending to their impromptu coffee
klatch had disconcerted her. Especially since he'd
gone out of his way to look her up, making it clear
that he wanted to talk with her, spend time with her.

The fact that he'd cut their conversation short didn't make sense, either.

And finally, her impulsive offer of a lift had *especially* not made sense.

Then again, not much in her life *had* made sense these past few weeks, she acknowledged with a sigh. Feelings she thought she'd sorted out long ago had bubbled to the surface. Especially her feelings about Scott. With each encounter, she became less able to sustain the hate that her father, particularly, still harbored—and encouraged. She understood her parents' feelings, of course. Had shared them until recently. In fact, in many ways hate made life easier. Fix the blame, condemn and walk away unblemished. It was much neater than sorting through messy shades of gray. But in reality, most situations just weren't that simple. Particularly this one, Jess was beginning to realize.

She let her head drop back and wearily closed her eyes. Since Elizabeth's death, fatigue had been her constant companion. Hate might make life easier by dulling the pain of grief, but maintaining such a draining and nonproductive emotion took a lot of energy. Especially now. It had been much easier to despise Scott when he was far removed and locked behind bars. It was a whole lot harder when he stood inches away and she saw nothing but kindness reflected in his eyes. Her resolve to keep him at arm's length was definitely wavering, she acknowledged. But was it because giving Scott a hearing was the right thing to do, as Mark had suggested—or because she was simply too tired to fight his clear, if unspoken, determination to once more be a part of her life?

Jess didn't know. And there was no one she could turn to for advice. Her parents were too biased against Scott to view the situation impartially. Mark was too much of an advocate on the other side. Which left her stuck in the middle. And directionless.

There was a time, of course, when she could have turned to Someone else for guidance, she reflected sadly. But that had been years ago, when God's presence had been a real part of her life. The connection between them had been broken long ago, and restoring it seemed an impossible task at this point. She didn't even know where to start. And until she did, she was on her own, with nothing to guide her but her instincts. Which she didn't have a whole lot of faith in, considering where they had led her today, she acknowledged ruefully.

A sudden knock on the passenger window brought her abruptly back to reality, and her head snapped up. She reached to unlock the door for Scott, leaning over even farther to push it open when she saw that he was juggling a small bakery box and a bouquet of flowers.

"Sorry. Were you sleeping?" he asked as he slid inside.

His shirt was damp, and she wondered how long he'd stood in the rain debating whether or not to disturb her. "No. Just resting."

"Long week?"

"Busy," she amended.

He gazed at her, noting that the shadows under her eyes seemed even deeper than when he'd first seen her weeks before. "You look tired, Jess," he said gently. "Are you sleeping okay?"

She gave him a startled look, and her eyes shuttered slightly. *Too personal,* Scott chided himself. *Back off.* "Sorry. None of my business."

She reached forward and turned on the motor, ignoring his comment. "Pretty flowers," she said as she looked over her shoulder and began backing out of the parking space.

"Yeah. I think she'll like them."

Jess's foot slipped off the brake and she almost ran into the car next to her.

"Careful!" he warned in alarm. "You're pretty close on this side. It's a tight spot. Just ease back and I'll let you know when you're clear."

Jess forced herself to concentrate on the task at hand. She didn't speak again until she was safely heading for the exit, and then she chose her words carefully, fishing but trying not to be obvious about it. "Looks like you're going to a party," she remarked, nodding toward the box in which a small cake was revealed beneath a clear window.

"Hardly. The cake and flowers are for an old woman in my apartment building. Take a right," he instructed as she reached the exit, then waited until she was safely in traffic before continuing. "I found her crying this morning on the stoop. It's her birthday, and apparently there's no one left who remembers. Her husband died years ago, and she hasn't heard from her son in a long time. So I thought I'd surprise her with flowers and share a piece of cake with her. It's not much, and it won't make up for her being alone, but maybe it will brighten her day for a few minutes at least. Take a left.''

Jess did as instructed, still processing the information Scott had just relayed. Though his tone had been low-key and matter-of-fact, his kindness was anything but, she conceded. He'd gone out of his way to remember a lonely old woman's birthday, spending money he obviously couldn't spare to give her a few moments of happiness. To let her know that someone cared.

Jess wasn't exactly surprised by Scott's thoughtfulness and generosity. He had always lavished gifts on her and Elizabeth—especially as the demands of his job left him unable to give them what they really wanted: his time. But his gifts had been well within their budget, given out of their excess. This gesture, on the other hand, was a gift out of his need. A living illustration of the widow's mite, Jess realized, deeply touched. Even more remarkable, it was for a woman who was practically a stranger, whose life had no connection to his beyond simple human compassion.

''This is it, the red one,'' he said, interrupting her thoughts.

Jess hadn't been paying much attention to her surroundings during the short drive to his apartment, but now she took a good look as she pulled up to the curb. And that's when she realized just how deep Scott's need was. The neighborhood he called home was not one she would feel comfortable in at high noon, let alone after dark. There was an abandoned building on the corner, and the apartments were housed in four-family flats that looked as if they'd been built at the turn of the century—and hadn't been updated since. Litter was strewn about on an abandoned lot across the street, and the lawn of the redbrick flat Scott occupied had more bare patches than grass. "Seedy" was the best way to describe the setting. "Dangerous" was a close second.

Jess stared at the neighborhood, appalled. This wasn't Scott. Not the Scott she'd married, whose wants were simple but who worked hard to provide his family with a decent standard of living. And certainly not the Scott who'd gone to prison, who had valued designer jeans and fine wines. Dear God, how could he live in these conditions? She turned to him in dismay, speechless, her shock clearly reflected in her eyes.

As their gazes met, Scott was instantly sorry he'd taken Jess up on her offer of a ride. The opportunity to spend additional time in her company—at *her* request—had simply been too tempting to refuse. But he should have anticipated her reaction. Should have known that it would be very similar to Karen's. His sister was *still* on him about the apartment, urging him to find other lodging. Offering to send him money. But as he kept telling her, it was good enough for now. In time, when he could afford it, he'd move. Until then, he'd sit tight and make the best of it. But Jess didn't need to hang around in a place like this, he decided, reaching for the door.

"Thanks again for the lift. And have a great time in Texas." He had already opened the door when her voice stopped him.

"Scott, wait. I...I didn't know that you...this is..."

She glanced again at the shabby surroundings and her voice died.

"Serviceable," he supplied evenly.

"Awful," she corrected him vehemently, the revulsion in her eyes clear.

"It beats a cell, Jess," he said quietly.

The comment jolted her, and she stared at him in stunned silence as their gazes connected and held. For the first time she had a sense at some primal level of the horror of incarceration. Of being in a place where you had no control over your existence, where you were told what to do and when to do it, where doors clanged shut behind you every night, leaving you to face your private demons alone in the darkness of a cold, sterile cell. Suddenly she understood how, in light of that existence, this squalid apartment would be an improvement. And all at once, a place in her heart that had long been numb and lifeless began to stir.

Her throat constricted with emotion and she swallowed with difficulty. "Scott, I had no idea. I'm..." She stopped abruptly, realizing in confusion that she'd almost said, "I'm sorry." But why was she sorry? Hadn't she believed all along that no punishment was too severe for what he'd done to Elizabeth?

Scott saw the parade of emotions pass across Jess's eyes. Compassion. Sympathy. Confusion. But no coldness. Or hate. Not this time. Which was progress as far as he was concerned. And so was her shock at his living conditions, he suddenly realized. After all, if she didn't have *some* feelings for him, she wouldn't care where he lived—would she?

"It's okay, Jess," he said with a gentle smile, his heart suddenly lighter. "I'm fine here. Really. I'm free. And I'm a person again, not a number. That makes any place seem like a palace. Trust me."

Jess didn't trust anything at the moment. Particularly her emotions. She had a sudden, desperate need to get away from here, to think this through alone, with no distractions. Especially the one sitting next to her.

"I have to go," she said in a choked voice, struggling to hold her tattered emotions together.

He studied her for a moment, his gaze penetrating and probing, and then he nodded. "I understand." Without further delay, he opened the door and stepped outside. "Thanks again, Jess. Take care."

She had no voice left to respond. She simply put the car in gear and drove away as quickly as she could, her stomach churning. But as she turned the corner, she couldn't resist the urge to look back. Scott was still standing where she had left him, watching her car disappear, holding the cake and flowers that would brighten an old woman's day. A ragged sob rose in her throat, and she had to blink rapidly to clear the sudden tears that blurred her vision. This was *not* the outcome she had expected from her encounter with Scott. Instead of helping her sort through her emotions, it had left her more confused than ever—and certain of only two things.

First, Scott *did* understand. Far too much. She'd seen it in his eyes. And that disturbed her greatly.

But even more disturbing was the fact that it had

taken every ounce of her willpower to drive away and leave him alone in that dismal place.

"Now, that's what I call the life of Riley."

At her brother's teasing voice, Jess's eyes flew open. "Mark! You made it!" she said in delight, scrambling to her feet to throw her arms around him.

He returned the bear hug, then, still holding her hands, backed off slightly to look her over. "Well, I have to say the Texas sun seems to be good for you."

"Lying around on a beach being lazy in a gorgeous place like Padre Island would be good for anyone. How long can you stay?"

"Just until Wednesday. I barely got away as it is. It was touch and go up until the last minute."

Jess wrinkled her nose. "Three days isn't long enough to relax."

"Tell that to my boss."

"You work too hard, Mark."

"I like what I do."

"You need time for other things."

"Such as?"

"Family."

"I'm here, aren't I?" he said, spreading out a towel on the sand, then flopping down. "I always make it for at least a couple days of the annual family vacation. Speaking of which—remember all those trips we took in the camper?" he said with a chuckle.

"And all the times we put it up in the rain," she replied, smiling ruefully as she sat on her towel and wrapped her arms around her knees.

"Yeah. Listen, don't tell Dad, but I much prefer the

condo," Mark admitted with a grin as he adjusted his sunglasses.

"I agree. Anyway, don't try to change the subject. You need time in your life for other things beside work."

"Like what?"

"A wife might be nice."

"There's plenty of time," he said nonchalantly. "Besides, I didn't come out here to talk about me. I want to hear all about you. And Scott. Mom doesn't seem to know anything, and you aren't exactly forthcoming on the phone."

Jess shrugged. "There's not much to tell."

He studied her for a moment, then shook his head. "Sorry. Don't buy it. We lived in the same house for more than twenty years. I can read you like a book."

"Baloney," she retorted, stretching out on the towel.

"Uh-uh," he said, leaning over to tickle the bottom of her foot. "You aren't getting off that easily."

"Stop that!" she said, swatting at him.

"Nope. Not till I get the truth."

She sat back up and crossed her legs. "How old did you say you were?" she demanded, trying to look stern.

"Thirty-one. Going on ten," he replied with an impudent grin.

"I believe it."

"So let's have the scoop on Scott. Have you taken my advice yet?"

"What makes you think I will?" she hedged.

"You'll bow to my superior wisdom in time," he said loftily, but the twinkle in his eyes belied his tone.

"You know, I think I'm beginning to understand why you're not married," she said sweetly, making a face at him.

"Hey! Let's not get personal!"

"I agree. Let's not." She lay back down and settled her sunglasses on her nose.

He gave her a moment's peace before trying a different tack. "Okay, fine. Have it your way. But how often do you get such a willing ear? Here I am, ready to put all my Listening 101 skills into action, and you're shutting me out."

She lifted her glasses and looked at him. "You aren't going to give up, are you?"

"Nope."

With a resigned sigh she sat up again. "So what do you want to know?"

"Everything."

"Let's not get too ambitious."

"Okay, okay. At least tell me if you've talked with him."

She eyed him warily. "First, a ground rule. This conversation stays between us. Agreed?"

"Sure."

She took a deep breath. "Yes, I've talked to him. Not about anything too serious. But our paths have crossed on a number of occasions—which Mom and Dad do not know about, by the way—and we've exchanged a few words. I also gave him a ride once. Now you have the whole story."

"How is he?"

Jess frowned. "He looks older. But he seems to have found...I don't know how to describe it, exactly. An inner peace, maybe. I do know that he's close friends with a local minister who's also one of the prison chaplains. He seems to have found a lot of comfort in his faith."

Mark's face registered surprise. "Really? I never thought Scott was all that religious. I mean, I know he went to church and lived a good life, but I never got the sense that he had a deep spiritual life."

"He seems to now."

"That's kind of ironic, isn't it?" Mark reflected. "In the midst of tragedy you lost God, and Scott found Him. Strange how life works. So how do you feel about this whole situation?"

"Honestly? Scared."

"I think that's probably normal."

Jess gazed out over the shimmering blue water. "I'm not sure I know what that word means anymore," she said wearily.

"I can tell you what it doesn't mean," Mark replied. "It doesn't mean keeping your feelings bottled inside. It doesn't mean ignoring issues. It doesn't mean pretending that everything's all right when it's not."

"You think that's what I've been doing?"

"I'd put money on it. How are you feeling about Scott these days?"

"Confused."

"Do you still hate him?"

"I keep trying to. But it...it gets harder and harder. Yet it seems somehow wrong to have anything to do with him. As if I'm...I don't know...dishonoring the memory of Elizabeth in some way.''

''Maybe the best way to honor her memory is with joy and forgiveness, not bitterness and hate,'' Mark said quietly. ''Scott loved her, Jess. Yet because of him, she died. He has to live with that every day of his life. Think of the pain and suffering he's already endured. What will it serve to add to that?''

''But I can't forget what happened, Mark.''

''We don't have to forget in order to forgive.''

''You make it sound simple.''

''Hardly. But you'll find some good guidelines in that Bible peeking out of your beach bag. Try Ephesians, chapter four, verses thirty-one and thirty-two.''

A flush rose on her cheeks, and she reached over and tucked the Bible out of sight. ''I haven't opened it in years. I'm not even sure why I brought it with me,'' she said dismissively.

''Personally, I think it was a good idea. Try Colossians, too. Chapter three, verses twelve through fourteen.''

She stared at him. ''Since when have you become such a Bible scholar?''

He shrugged. ''Let's just say that I've been on my own journey. And I want you to know that...'' He shifted uncomfortably. ''Well, along the way I've been praying for you and Scott.''

Her throat constricted with emotion at this rare display of what her brother usually called ''mushy stuff.'' ''Thanks, Mark.''

''Hey, what are brothers for?'' he said with a grin

as he stretched out on his towel, once more his irreverent self. "Call me for advice anytime."

"Let all bitterness, and wrath, and indignation, and clamor, and reviling, be removed from you, along with all malice. On the contrary, be kind to one another, and merciful, generously forgiving one another, as also God in Christ has generously forgiven you."

Jess read the words twice, then turned to the second passage her brother had suggested.

"Put on therefore, as God's chosen ones, holy and beloved, a heart of mercy, kindness, humility, meekness, patience. Bear with one another and forgive one another, if anyone has a grievance against any other; even as the Lord has forgiven you, so also do you forgive. But above all these things have love, which is the bond of perfection."

Slowly she closed the book and lay back on her pillow. She'd spoken truthfully to Mark when she'd said she had no idea why she'd brought her Bible on vacation. Especially since she hadn't opened it in almost four years. It had been a last-minute addition to her luggage, and she hadn't looked at it all week. But something had compelled her to include it.

No, that wasn't entirely true, she acknowledged. It wasn't some*thing,* but some*one.* Namely, Scott. He seemed to have found his way through the labyrinth of pain and grief of the past few years far better than she had. She could see reflected in his eyes the very things her soul desperately longed for. Acceptance of what life had dealt him. Understanding that gave clarity to chaos. A clear and confident sense of direction and destination. A perspective that tempered sadness with trust. He was clearly a man who had made his peace with himself and with his God and, in so doing, had found hope for tomorrow. And the Bible had apparently played a key role in his journey. Because that's where Scott seemed to go for comfort and guidance.

But he didn't just read the Bible. He clearly had an ongoing dialogue with the Lord, Jess acknowledged. His words to God in the cemetery had been a relaxed conversation rather than a stilted, formal prayer, suggesting that he was accustomed to speaking to the Lord on a very personal level. Even when Jess had considered her faith to be at its strongest, she'd never reached the spiritual depth, the personal relationship with God, that Scott now seemed to enjoy.

Because of that relationship, she had a feeling that although he was probably as lonely as she was in many ways, he never felt truly alone. And she envied him that. Even the love of her parents hadn't been able to assuage the terrible, desolate sense of aloneness that had darkened her days for the past four years. Something was missing from her life, something more than her beloved Elizabeth or the husband she had once adored. The loss was even more profound than that, and she felt it at the very depths of her soul. It was a sense of isolation—and separation—from the one unchanging reality of life. From God.

Her throat constricted with emotion, and Jess closed her eyes. Mark had been right earlier in the day when he'd noted the irony that Scott, the less ''religious'' of the two, had found his way out of the maze of despair through faith, while Jess stumbled around in darkness, her bitterness toward God and her husband twisting her heart with a malignant anger. Scott had resolved his issues, while Jess's had simply festered. And he'd done it with the help of the God Jess had turned her back on. The God she had railed against in pain and anguish for taking her beloved daughter. The God she had abandoned as uncaring and unfair. Yet in his need, Scott had found in that very same God a loving, forgiving Father who stretched out His hand to those who called upon Him for help.

Jess knew that her rejection of the Lord had been motivated by anger and an inability to comprehend how a good and loving God could allow such tragic events to occur. She'd tortured herself over and over again asking "why?" and seeking answers where there were none. But as was slowly becoming clear to her, discerning the purposes of the Lord was a task far beyond the limited powers of the human intellect. After all, the Lord never called on us to understand His ways—just to accept them. And to trust in His abiding love.

That's what Scott had done. What Jess *needed* to do. Because she now realized that until she, too, found her way back to the Lord, she would never achieve the peace, and the healing, that Scott had found.

At the same time, she knew that it wouldn't be easy. Because the Bible verses Mark had recommended made it clear that though God was always ready to forgive us, He expected us to follow His example. Meaning that if Jess truly wanted to find her way back to the Lord, she needed to forgive, as well. And she would need a lot of help with that, she acknowledged. She needed God. But how did one begin to rebuild a relationship with the Almighty?

Jess turned back to the Bible and idly let it fall open. The words from James that met her eyes provided the answer to her question so clearly that for a moment she simply sat there in stunned silence.

"Draw near to God and He will draw near to you."

It sounded so easy, she thought. And perhaps it was. Perhaps it was as simple as what Scott had done in the cemetery, when he'd simply talked with the Lord. It was certainly worth a try. Jess drew in a steadying breath, then let her eyelids drift closed. And though she felt as tentative and awkward as a baby taking its first steps, she began to speak haltingly in the silence of her heart.

Dear Lord, I know that I've been away from You for…well, for too long. I don't know how to find my way back…only that I need to, because my soul is hungry for the peace that I see in Scott's eyes, a peace that I now know only comes from You. He's changed so much, Lord. For the better. And I believe with all my heart that it's because he found his way back to You. I'd like to do the same. I ask for Your help and Your grace, and for Your loving hand to guide me in right paths as I begin this journey. Most of all, I ask Your forgiveness for turning away from You in bitterness and anger. And I ask You to help me find in my heart the forgiveness that You so generously offer to all who seek it from You—and without which true healing can never occur.

When she finished her prayer, Jess drew a long,

shaky breath. She knew that there was much more she could say. More that she could confess. More that she could ask. But this was a start.

Jess hadn't expected any immediate guidance. And none was forthcoming. Yet she no longer felt quite so alone. Because although the Lord's voice was quiet at the moment, she sensed that He was listening.

And she would do the same.

Chapter Eight

"Are you sure about driving me home, Dad? I can just stay in the cab and save you a trip."

"Don't even think about it, dear," said Clare. "Your father doesn't mind giving you a lift. We'll just transfer your luggage to our car."

"Welcome home, Clare, Frank. Hello, Jess. Did you have a good time?"

Frank paid the cabdriver, then turned to greet his neighbor. "Hello, David. Padre Island is always great. Everything okay here?"

"Just fine now, but we had a bad storm the day after you left. Saturday afternoon. Blew in here with a vengeance. We lost power for fourteen hours, and there were trees down all over the place."

Frank frowned, then turned to Clare and Jess. "I'll get the luggage in a minute. I better go check the roses."

"They're fine," David assured him. "They took a beating, but a nice young man came by bright and early Sunday morning and cleaned everything up. You'd hardly know there was even a storm.''

Frank's frown deepened. ''Who was it?''

''Can't say I've ever seen him before,'' David replied. ''Of course, Marge and I have only lived here a couple of years, but he said he'd known you for a long time. When I asked his name, he just smiled and said he was a Good Samaritan. I kind of got the impression that he'd just as soon have done his good deed and gone on his way without being noticed. But I figured you'd want to know.''

Jess stared at the man as a suspicion began to niggle at her brain. Could *Scott* have been the Good Samaritan? Knowing how much her father's roses meant to him, and despite his less-than-kind treatment at the garden, had Scott nonetheless stepped in to help?

''What did he look like, David?'' Frank asked.

''Tall. Good shape. Dark hair. A little silver at the temples, now that I think about it. So maybe he wasn't quite so young after all.''

Jess's suspicion changed to certainty.

''I'll bring your mail over a little later,'' David continued. ''Now I'll leave you folks alone to unpack and get settled.''

''Isn't that odd, Frank?'' Clare gave her husband a puzzled look as their neighbor strolled back to his house. ''Who on earth would have done such a thing?''

Jess drew a deep, steadying breath. ''It was Scott.''

As she had expected, both heads swiveled in her direction and her parents stared at her in shocked silence for several long moments. Finally her father found his voice.

"What makes you say that?" There was a note of caution—and distance—in his tone.

Jess swallowed and nervously tucked her hair behind her ear. "I think maybe we better go inside so I can explain."

Frank nodded curtly and reached for two suitcases. "Good idea. No sense airing family business in public. If you ladies can get those carry-ons, we should be able to do this in one trip."

Once inside, Frank wasted no time getting back to the matter at hand. He dropped the bags in the living room, then turned to his daughter. "Okay, Jess. What do you know about this?"

"Why don't we sit down?" she suggested, her heart thumping painfully in her chest. She should have known that eventually her parents would find out that she had talked with Scott. It had been silly to keep it a secret. And it made things very awkward now.

"I don't feel like sitting," Frank replied, propping his fists on his hips. "You've been seeing him, haven't you?" he said accusatorily.

Clare stared at her daughter. "Is that true, Jess?"

Jess took a deep breath. "Not exactly. But our paths have crossed by chance on several occasions and…" A skeptical snort from her father made her voice falter.

"Frank, let Jess tell us the story," Clare admonished him before sitting down across from her daughter. "Go on, honey."

"Our meetings *were* by chance," Jess repeated more forcefully. "He works for a landscaping company, and I happened to be passing two of the job sites he was assigned to. I also ran into him at the cemetery on Elizabeth's birthday. And I saw him one day at the garden.''

"I didn't know you still went to the cemetery," Clare said gently.

Frank brushed past that. "Do you mean you saw him at the garden other than the time we all ran into him?"

"Yes. About a week later. He asked about your roses, and I told him that you'd gotten into them in a big way. How you enter shows and everything. I also mentioned that we were leaving on vacation, so I guess he put two and two together, figured we were gone and decided to come over and attend to the roses after the storm. Which probably took a lot of effort, because he doesn't have a car. He must have taken the bus.''

Frank frowned. "How do you know he doesn't have a car?"

"He told me. The day I ran into him at the garden." She frowned. "Dad, did you know that Scott turned everything over to me when he went to prison? Every dime?"

"Yes. It was the least he could do after ruining your life," Frank replied coldly. "We discussed it at the time."

Twin furrows creased Jess's brow. "I guess I didn't pay much attention. Money was the last thing on my mind. I always just assumed he kept *something* in reserve for when he got out. But he didn't. You should see how he lives.''

Frank's frown of disapproval deepened. "How do you know how he lives?"

Jess felt hot color creep up her neck. She was getting in deeper and deeper. "I...I gave him a ride home from the garden. It was raining." She turned to her mother, hoping for an ally. "Mom, it's a terrible neighborhood. Run-down and dangerous looking."

Clare shook her head. "I don't know what to say, Jess," she replied helplessly. "I thought you hated Scott. But now...well, your attitude seems almost...sympathetic."

"Frankly, I don't know how I feel anymore," she admitted with a sigh. "He's changed so much. For the better. I can see it in his eyes. There's a remarkable humbleness and peace about him. And kindness. Look what he just did for you, Dad."

"He probably had an ulterior motive," her father replied brusquely. "Maybe he thought it was a way to get to *you.*"

"That's a pretty cynical attitude."

"I'd call it cautious," he countered stubbornly. "Why else would he do me a favor, except to build up brownie points with you? I've made it pretty clear to him how I feel. So have you—at least, until recently. So what's his motivation?"

Love. He's doing it because he still loves me.

The thought came unbidden, and left Jess momentarily stunned—and speechless.

Suddenly Frank's eyes narrowed. "You know, if his living conditions are as bad as you say, maybe he's having second thoughts about turning all his assets over to you. Maybe he's after money."

The comment jolted Jess back to reality and she stared at him, appalled. "That's a terrible thing to say, Dad!"

"I wouldn't put it past him," he persisted, his voice laced with derision.

"But how can you think that?" Jess demanded in dismay. "Scott made some bad *mistakes,* but he was never a bad *man.* Or mercenary. Or dishonest."

Her father's eyes grew cold. "No. He was just a murderer."

The bitterness in her father's voice was so venomous that Jess actually flinched. She knew her father hated Scott. But surely his hatred hadn't always been this virulent. Or had she simply been so caught up in her own pain that she'd never fully grasped the intensity of his feelings?

"Frank...those are pretty harsh words," Clare said in gentle reproach.

He turned to her. "Are you getting soft, too? That man killed your granddaughter, for God's sake! And almost ruined your daughter's life."

Clare flushed. "I know. But...well, he didn't do it on purpose, Frank. And he did go to prison."

"I suppose that makes up for everything," he replied sarcastically.

"No. But what would?"

Her mother's quiet, insightful question silenced her father for a moment, and Jess took the opportunity to reach for her purse and stand up. "I need to get home."

Frank nodded stiffly. "I'll get the car."

"Maybe I should take a cab, Dad."

Frank sighed and raked his fingers through his thick head of gray hair. "No. I'll drive you. No sense letting this thing disrupt the family. But I have a bad feeling about this, Jess. I think reestablishing contact with Scott is a mistake. You're opening the door to a lot of things that are best left buried."

She sighed. "That's the trouble, Dad. I'm beginning to realize that burying problems doesn't make them go away. And that maybe it's time I dealt with them."

Jess entered the dimly lit auditorium and made her way inconspicuously along the back wall, scanning the last few rows of the seemingly packed house for an empty seat. She'd had no idea that religious retreats were such a big draw, she thought incredulously. Then again, perhaps the theme was responsible for the crowd. Maybe a lot of people were seeking guidance on how to cope with adversity.

Though Jess hadn't planned to attend the event, something had compelled her to keep the flyer. Then, when she'd returned from vacation, she'd dug it out of the drawer where she had carelessly tossed it. Now that she had begun to pray for the courage and strength to forgive, it seemed like a good idea to hear what Scott had to say. Not that she intended to make her presence known. This was simply a fact-finding mission. A chance to hear his story from the anonymity of a darkened auditorium. An opportunity to view the situation from a different perspective and perhaps gain some insight that would help her understand her feelings.

So far, perspective and insight had eluded her, she

acknowledged. Every time she'd seen Scott since his release, she'd been so busy trying to control her turbulent emotions, so focused on carrying on a rational conversation that she hadn't really been able to focus on *him*. She needed an opportunity to study him unobserved and unselfconsciously so that she could get a better handle on who he was now, this man who was still her husband and whom she had once known intimately, but who had changed in some dramatic, fundamental way. That's what tonight's outing was all about. She'd planned it down to the minute: arrive just in time for Scott's remarks, which were the last item on the agenda, sit in the back, then slip out unnoticed as soon as his talk ended.

Well, she'd arrived at the right time. But the sitting part didn't look too promising. However, just when she was about to give up she came upon a single empty seat in the last row. With a sigh of relief and a murmured apology, she edged past a couple of people and sank into the chair just as a sandy-haired, fiftyish minister with a kind face stepped to the podium.

"Ladies and gentlemen, for those of you who don't know me, I'm Reverend Keith Young," he said in a pleasant, well-modulated voice. "Let me add my own words of welcome on behalf of all the sponsoring churches, and thank you for your support of this wonderful event.

"For the last few hours, a number of highly respected Bible scholars have talked to us about the guidance offered in Scripture for dealing with adversity. And we've heard a number of amazing first-person stories about the healing and transforming power of faith. While all of the stories are inspiring, we've saved perhaps the most *dramatic* story until last.

"I met our next speaker, Scott Mitchell, about three years ago when he was in prison serving time for vehicular manslaughter. Scott had been involved in a drunk-driving accident in which two people were killed—a judge and his own four-year-old daughter."

A hushed murmur ran through the crowd, and the minister waited for it to subside before continuing.

"That night changed Scott's life forever. Today he has agreed to share with you his remarkable journey from grief and despair to redemption and hope. Please give Scott a warm welcome."

As the audience applauded, Scott rose from a seat in the front row and made his way to the slightly elevated platform, where the two men shook hands warmly. Then the minister placed his left hand on Scott's shoulder and said something quietly. Scott nodded, and as Reverend Young returned to his seat, Scott set the Bible he was carrying on the podium and reached for the microphone.

For a long moment he simply looked out over the group in silence, as if gathering his thoughts. Then he took a deep breath and began to speak.

"Once upon a time, in a different world, when I was a different man, I used to stand up in front of large groups of people all the time to give presentations on advertising campaigns and focus groups and consumer preferences," he said quietly. His voice was calm and in control, but Jess heard the husky undertones, a clear sign to anyone who knew him well that his emotions were close to the surface. Curiously, it wasn't a tone she had ever heard him use in public. He'd always been guarded about exposing his feelings to anyone except close family. Had he changed in that regard, too? she wondered, intrigued.

"In those days, I wore expensive suits and drove an expensive car and drank expensive liquor," he continued. "I traveled first class, ate in the best restaurants, mingled with the right people. Everyone thought I had it all. Including me. But my wife, Jess, knew better."

At the mention of her name, Jess drew in a sharp breath, and her heart began to thump painfully.

"Jess saw right through all the 'stuff' I grew to value so highly. She recognized it for what it was—a distraction from what really counted. Namely love. And friendship. And family. And simple pleasures. And faith. She tried to help me see that, too, because she recognized that our diverging values were causing problems in our marriage. But instead of listening, I started drinking. Not enough to be an alcoholic, but too much at times. Especially one particular time. The night my world ended."

Scott paused, and Jess saw his Adam's apple bob convulsively. The stark pain on his face was a window to the torment his soul had endured, and her throat constricted with emotion as memories of that night came swirling back to her as well, out of the dark recesses of her mind to which she'd banished them.

Scott moved to a stool in the center of the stage and perched on the edge, resting one foot on a rung. He drew a deep breath, and when he spoke again his voice was slightly unsteady.

"For the next few minutes I'd like to tell you what

happened to me after that night. But I have to be honest with you. I didn't want to come here today. I'm not a man who has always been especially good at opening up to people and sharing my feelings. However, Reverend Young can be persuasive. He convinced me that maybe someone might be able to find in what I have to say a ray of hope that will give them the courage to carry on. And once he convinced me of that, I couldn't say no. Because I know how empty life can be without hope. So I'll give it my best.''

And for the next forty-five minutes he did exactly that. He spoke of the horrors of the accident, in which he escaped unscathed while his wife suffered a concussion and two people died, including his beloved Elizabeth. He spoke of the surreal cemetery scene, choking up as he talked about kneeling beside the small white coffin as his world crashed in around him. He spoke briefly of the trial, how he went through the motions numbly, still in a state of shock.

He spoke at length about prison...of the suffocating feeling that accompanied the loss of freedom...of the degradation of being treated like a number instead of a person...of the long, empty days marked by rigid, repetitive routine. He spoke in a ragged voice of the pain and anguish and grief that struck fiercely once the numbness wore off. And he spoke of the crushing guilt that squeezed the life from his soul. Of the aching void left in his heart after the death of his wife's love. Of the hopelessness and despair and emptiness that drove him to such depths of depression that at times he felt suicidal. Of how he would lie in his dark cell at night, tears running down his face, praying for God to simply end his agony.

"I wanted to die," Scott said, his voice choked and raw with emotion. "I'd lost my daughter. My wife. My freedom. My self-respect. My identity. I was as low as you could get. And that's when Reverend Young came into my life."

He stood again and moved to the edge of the stage, closer to the audience, taking a moment to compose himself. "My faith had never been especially strong," he continued. "Certainly not strong enough to withstand the nightmare my life had become. I couldn't fathom how a loving God would wreak such havoc on me and on the people I loved. I'd gone through a brief anger phase, but by the time I met Reverend Young I was at a point where I just didn't care anymore. About anything. So he had his work cut out for him. Because anger is actually a lot easier to deal with than apathy.

"He didn't give up, though. Week after week, sometimes twice a week, he'd show up. At first we didn't even talk about religion. But gradually he began to work that into the conversation. And one day he gave me this." Scott reached for the well-thumbed Bible and held it up. "He had marked a passage he thought I might find helpful, and even though I told him I wasn't interested, he left the book with me. Since time hangs heavy on your hands in prison, I ended up paging through it one day simply out of desperation for something to do. And the passage he had marked seemed to speak directly to me."

Scott opened the book and read. "'Only in God be at rest, my soul, for from Him comes my hope.'"

He paused for a moment, then closed the book and looked out at the audience. "Reverend Young, in his wisdom, had pointed me to the two things I needed most desperately—rest and hope. Guilt and self-recrimination are terrible burdens that can eat away at you like a cancer and rob life of all peace and hope. But with Reverend Young's help, I eventually came to experience the healing power of God's forgiveness. To understand that He always stands ready to absolve us if we truly repent. And that He never deserts us. For as He told us, He is with us always, even to the end of time. And as He also promised, all things are possible with Him.

"I stand before you tonight as a living testament to the healing power of God's forgiveness and hope," Scott said with quiet sincerity. "I didn't reach this place overnight. It was a long, hard struggle, and I'm sure there were times when Reverend Young was ready to give up on me." He directed a brief smile toward the minister. "But I can tell you that the rewards are great for those who persevere, who seek the Lord with an open mind and open heart, and who are willing to put their trust in Him and listen to His words.

"When Reverend Young asked me to speak today, I told him that I wasn't sure I was the best choice. That I'd made a lot of mistakes and that I'm not where I want to be yet. I guess you could say my life is in a reconstruction phase at this point. When I left prison, I had two goals. One was to make faith the center of my life, and that has been easy. The other, however, has been much more difficult. And that's to win back the love of my wife.''

As he paused to draw a deep breath, Jess suddenly felt as if all the air had been squeezed out of her own lungs.

''I realize that's an ambitious goal,'' Scott continued. ''But I'm working on it. I've put my trust in the Lord, and I'm following the advice in Proverbs, which tells us, 'In his mind a man plans his course, but the Lord directs his steps.' Well, I know what my plan is. I love my wife with a passion and intensity that has grown rather than diminished through our years of separation, and I can't even imagine the rest of my life without her. So I trust that the Lord will guide me as I seek my goal.

''You know, a very wise man once told me that even on the coldest, darkest days of winter it's important to remember that spring always comes. I believe that with all my heart. And with the Lord's help, I have great faith that my life will once again bloom and bear fruit. Thank you.''

There was a moment of silence, and then the auditorium was filled with thunderous applause as the audience rose to its feet in a resounding ovation. Jess followed suit, reaching up to self-consciously brush away the tears that were streaming down her face. But when she glanced around, she realized that she wasn't alone in her reaction. With his humble manner, painfully honest revelations and inspiring message of hope, Scott had clearly touched many hearts in this room. Including hers.

But beyond that, Scott's talk had also surprised her.

Knowing how guarded he usually was when it came to talking about his feelings, she'd assumed that his presentation today would be a relatively straightforward account of his life in prison and a fairly sedate faith witness. Instead, he had spoken from the heart, exposing his deepest feelings and baring his soul to this room of strangers. Because of his willingness to share so openly, he'd connected with the audience at the deepest of levels, and in so doing had made every person in the room experience his pain and desolation in an almost tangible way. Likewise, his faith witness had been inspiring, offering hope that even the bleakest situation can be overcome through trust in the Lord.

Like everyone else in the audience, Jess had been deeply impressed and profoundly moved. But unlike them, she was suddenly afraid. Because if her previous encounters with Scott had shaken the foundations of the wall between them, tonight's revealing testimonial had knocked a gaping hole in it, opening a passage directly to her heart. And as the protective barrier she had erected between them crumbled, she felt increasingly exposed and vulnerable. It was risky business, this notion of reconnecting and forgiving, Jess realized, and she prayed that she had the strength to see it through.

When the applause at last died down and people once more took their seats, Reverend Young moved back to the podium. He paused to embrace Scott, and the warmth between the two men was unmistakable. Another first, Jess noted. Scott had always avoided public displays of affection, but he seemed totally comfortable with them now.

As the minister began to speak, Jess knew it was time to leave. She didn't want to run the risk of encountering Scott until she'd had time to sort through her turbulent emotions. With a murmured apology, she edged past several people and headed toward the exit, determined to make a hasty retreat. However, her step faltered when a ladies'-room sign caught her eye. She glanced uncertainly toward the stage, where Reverend Young seemed to be in the midst of his concluding remarks. Surely there would be time for a quick visit, she thought, changing directions.

But Jess had miscalculated. When she pushed the door open less than four minutes later the audience was on its feet, and quite a few people were already passing the ladies' room on their way to the exit. The minister must have wrapped up his remarks in record time, she realized in dismay.

Jess glanced toward the front of the auditorium. She could see the top of Scott's head above the crowd as he moved toward the exit. Not good, she realized in panic, quickly stepping back.

Even though she felt foolish about being a prisoner in the ladies' room, Jess couldn't see any way out of her predicament. She wasn't ready to face Scott. So her only option was to wait until the place cleared.

A few women stopped in the ladies' room on their way out, and Jess made a pretense of touching up her lipstick and combing her hair. But gradually the visitors tapered off and the din of the crowd subsided.

Jess was just about to push the door open and peek out when voices on the other side stopped her.

"...was feeling worse and worse, so I told him to go home."

"No problem. I can catch a bus."

She froze. It was Scott. And Reverend Young.

"I don't know," the minister said skeptically. "It won't be easy at this time of day on a weekend. The schedule is so abbreviated." He sighed. "I didn't think this would be an issue when I sent Ray home. I planned to give you a ride myself until I got the page from the hospital."

"That's more important," Scott said firmly. "You need to be with that family. Don't worry about it. Trust me, I've gotten very good at this public transportation thing."

A third, unfamiliar voice joined the conversation, which moved to another topic. Jess frowned and took a deep breath. She had a feeling of déjà vu. Once more, Scott was without a ride—and she was in a position to help. But she didn't want to see him. Didn't want him to know about her presence at this event until she'd thought about all he'd said. At the same time, it seemed somehow selfish and uncharitable not to assist. As she wrestled with the dilemma, the third person said his goodbyes, once more leaving Scott and Reverend Young alone.

"You better head out, Reverend. I'll see you at services next week."

"All right, Scott. Thanks."

It was now or never. Without even giving herself a

chance for second thoughts, Jess followed her instincts and pushed open the ladies'-room door.

The two men were standing about ten feet away, and both glanced in her direction. Reverend Young gave her a pleasant look, but Scott's expression went at warp speed from mild interest to shock to incredulity.

"Jess?" His voice was tentative, as if he couldn't quite believe his eyes.

"Hello, Scott." Her own voice was none too steady—and neither were her legs, she realized as she forced herself to close the distance between them. Her gaze connected with Scott's, and the delight and welcome in his eyes sent a flush of color to her cheeks.

When neither of them spoke, the minister stepped in. "Jess, I'm Reverend Young. It's a pleasure to meet you at last."

With an effort Jess tore her gaze away from Scott's and reached out to find her hand taken in a warm clasp. "Hello, Reverend."

"I've heard a great deal about you. All good things, I might add."

Jess's flush deepened and she glanced at Scott, unsure how to respond. So instead she changed the subject. "I couldn't help overhearing your conversation," she said a bit breathlessly. "And I—I'd be glad to give you a ride home."

He smiled, and the warmth in his eyes spilled into her heart. "I appreciate the offer, Jess. But it's too far out of your way."

She shrugged. "I don't have any plans for tonight anyway."

Reverend Young chimed in. "I'd take her up on it, Scott. Buses are few and far between at this hour."

Scott looked at her again. "Are you sure?"

She nodded, though in fact she wasn't sure at all.

"Then I accept. Thank you."

"And thank you again, Scott," Reverend Young said, placing his hand on the younger man's shoulder. "You gave a powerful talk that I know will help more than a few people find strength in their faith and better equip them to cope with their own adversity."

"I'm glad you think it was worthwhile. But I'm also glad it's over," he admitted with a grin.

The minister chuckled. "I'm sure you are. And I'll see you next week." He turned to Jess and once more extended his hand. "It was good to finally meet you, Jess. Feel free to join us anytime for Sunday services. You'd be most welcome."

Jess watched the minister stride toward the exit. She could feel Scott's gaze on her, but it took her several moments to gather the courage to turn to him. And when she did, she was momentarily distracted by the way his sky-blue cotton shirt hugged his broad, muscular chest, and by the small V of dark, springy hair that was visible at the open neck. He was tanned and fit and looked very, very appealing, she realized as her pulse accelerated. An almost tangible virility radiated from him, literally taking her breath away.

"It's good to see you, Jess," he said quietly, his eyes smiling warmly into hers. "I had no idea you'd be here today. Or that you even knew about it."

"I—I'm still on the mailing list at my church," she

stammered, thrown off balance by her wayward thoughts. "I got a flyer."

He studied her for a moment. "I wish I'd known you were coming."

She looked at him curiously. "Why?"

"Because when a man professes his love for a woman, he usually likes to do it directly," Scott said softly, his burning gaze holding hers captive and making her heart lurch into triple time. "I didn't intend to tip my hand to you so soon about my intentions, but I guess God had different plans. So I'll have to go with the flow. I realize there's a lot that still divides us, and that it will take a miracle for you to forgive me, let alone find it in your heart to love me again. But I believe in miracles, Jess. And I have hope." He paused and took a deep breath. "So now you know how I feel."

She stared at him, taken aback by his sincere and straightforward declaration of love. She wished she was as clear about what *she* wanted and how *she* felt. But she was still confused and groping for answers. And she had no idea how to reply.

As if sensing her dilemma, Scott smiled gently. "I'm not asking for a response, Jess. Given what you heard today, I'm just grateful that you're willing to offer me a ride rather than telling me to take a hike. Shall we head out?"

Not trusting her voice, she simply nodded and led the way toward the exit. Scott fell into step beside her, and when they approached the door he reached past her to push it open. He was so close that his breath was warm on her temple and she could catch the distinctive male scent that was his alone. So close that a powerful surge of longing raced through her, catching her off guard and leaving her slightly breathless. So close that it reminded her of days long ago when a simple touch, or even a mere look, was enough to set off sparks that led to kisses—and often much more. Her mouth went dry, and when she risked a glance at Scott she found that the warmth in his gaze had been replaced by need. And unlike their encounter at the garden, when she thought she'd detected a flame of passion in his eyes before it was quickly masked, this time he made no attempt to hide it. He let her see exactly what was on his mind. Love. Attraction. Desire. Need.

Jess looked away quickly, more confused than ever. For years she'd thought that the passion she'd felt for Scott had died in the accident that robbed her of her cherished daughter. But she'd been surprised once in the garden, and again now, by its sudden and persistent resurgence. And she wasn't ready to deal with it. Or even think about it. Caution was the operative word here, she reminded herself. She knew exactly how Scott felt and what he wanted. Now she needed to logically figure out how *she* felt and what *she* wanted. She needed to analyze the situation rationally, without being influenced by hormones.

But unfortunately they were beginning to get in the way.

Chapter Nine

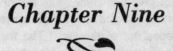

The ride to Scott's apartment was extremely awkward. At least for Jess. After thanking him for coming to the aid of her father's roses, she couldn't think of anything else to say. He, on the other hand, seemed to have no trouble making small talk, she thought enviously. Though she tried to take part, her responses sounded stiff and stilted even to her own ears.

All awkwardness and self-consciousness vanished, however, when Jess turned onto Scott's street and found their route blocked by emergency vehicles with flashing lights.

"This doesn't look good," she said with a frown as she pulled to a stop.

An officer from a nearby police car walked over, and Jess rolled down her window.

"Can I help you, ma'am?" he asked.

Scott leaned over. "I live near the end of the block, Officer." When he gave the address, the man frowned.

"I'm afraid that's where the problem was. Faulty

wiring in one of the flats started a fire. Fortunately, it was contained to one unit, but *unfortunately* I think it was yours." He took a notepad out of his pocket. "Are you Scott Mitchell?"

"Yes."

"I'm sorry, sir. There's not much left," he said sympathetically. "If you'll pull over to the curb, ma'am, I can give you some more information."

Jess did as he directed, and the officer rejoined them as they stepped out of the car. "The fire's been out for a couple of hours, so we're just about to wrap up here. We've moved everybody out temporarily."

"Was anyone hurt?" Scott asked in concern.

"No. Which probably wouldn't be the case if this had happened at night. This kind of fire catches quickly, and smoke inhalation is a real danger. So if there's a bright side, that's it. I can let you have a look if you'd like to try and salvage anything," he offered.

"Yes, thanks. I'll be right with you." The man nodded, and as he walked back toward his patrol car Scott turned to Jess. "Well, this is certainly an exciting end to the day," he said with a rueful smile. "But to be honest, dealing with a fire isn't half as bad as getting up in front of that roomful of people."

She stared at him, amazed at his calm acceptance of the situation and distraught by the unexpected turn of events.

"Hey, don't look like that," Scott said softly. He lifted his hand as if to reach out and touch her face, then let it fall back to his side. "Everything will be fine. So don't worry about it, okay? And thank you again for the ride. I appreciate it more than I can say."

She continued to stare at him. Did he actually think she was just going to go merrily on her way? His home—if such a generous term could be applied to his shabby flat—had just burned down! He had apparently lost everything. *She* was upset, even if he didn't seem to be. There was no way she could walk out on *anyone* in those straits. Especially Scott. Not after she'd listened to his story today. Not after everything he'd already gone through. Not after he'd made it clear that he loved her.

"I'll stay for a few minutes," she said. Before he could reply, she reached into the car for her purse and slung it over her shoulder.

When she turned back to him, the look in his eyes spoke more eloquently than words of his gratitude—and love. Silently he stepped aside to allow her to follow the officer, then fell in beside her, his hand protectively at her elbow. The light touch of his fingers on her bare skin was like an electric charge, and she tightened her grip on her purse, struggling to control the tremors that ran through her body. Scott might have tipped his hand today about his feelings, but she wasn't yet ready to acknowledge her own—to him, or to herself.

The officer stopped at the edge of the taped-off area and nodded toward what had been Scott's apartment. "The floors are okay, and structurally the building is still sound. These old places were built to last. But the walls and ceilings in your apartment are scorched and there's not much left of the contents."

"I'll just take a quick look around." Scott turned to Jess. "Will you be okay here for a few minutes?"

"I'll stick close," the officer promised.

"Thanks. Hang on to this for me, okay?" He handed Jess his Bible, then turned and strode toward the burned-out apartment.

"Tough break," the officer said, shaking his head sympathetically. "But he seems to be taking it okay. I hope he didn't have anything too valuable in there."

Jess doubted it. Mostly because he didn't seem to *have* anything valuable. At least not in a material sense.

The officer's radio crackled to life, and after a murmured "excuse me," he moved a few feet away to handle the call, leaving Jess alone to stare at the vacant building where most of Scott's unit had been reduced to ashes—just as his life had been, she thought, struck by the symbolism. She glanced thoughtfully down at the Bible she held in her hands, which had provided him with the comfort and courage to overcome tragedy and go on with his life—and with the perspective to understand what really counted. Maybe that's why the fire seemed of so little consequence to him, she mused. It had destroyed only things, which were replaceable. It hadn't destroyed anything of real value.

When Scott emerged a few minutes later he was carrying only a few items, and she looked at them curiously as he approached. There was a family picture of herself, Scott and Elizabeth, which had miraculously survived even if its frame had not; a small metal cross; and two books on horticulture that were a bit charred at the edges. That was it. Her throat tightened with emotion, and when her gaze rose to his, she had to forcibly resist the urge to reach up and wipe away a smudge of soot on his cheek.

He smiled at her, but she could see the weariness in his face, smell the acrid scent of smoke on his clothes. "The officer was right. There's not much left. I'm pretty much down to the clothes on my back."

"I'm sorry, Scott," she whispered.

"Hey, it's okay," he reassured her, forcing his lips into a smile. "I salvaged the only things that were really important to me. And I'm getting used to this starting-over thing. I'll be fine." He glanced toward the apartment, and it was clear when he spoke that the symbolism wasn't lost on him, either. "Maybe I'll be like the phoenix. Maybe something new will rise out of the ashes," he said quietly. He was silent for a moment, and when he turned back to her his grin was genuine. "Anyway, Karen won't be sorry. She hated this place."

"I can't say I blame her."

Scott shrugged. "It met my needs."

"Did you find anything worth saving?" the officer interrupted as he rejoined them.

"Not much," Scott admitted.

The man sighed. "I didn't think you would. Listen, you're welcome to use my phone if you need to call someone or arrange a place to spend the night."

"He can use my cell phone," Jess interjected.

"Okay. Then I just need to ask you a few questions for our report," the officer said to Scott. "I've got the paperwork in my car. Ma'am, you can wait in your car if you'd like. This won't take long."

She nodded, and they made their way silently back

down the block. Scott opened her door for her when they reached her car, and after she slipped into the driver's seat he leaned down.

"You don't need to wait, Jess. This might take a while, and I'm sure you have better things to do than hang around here."

She looked at him, this man she had long ago said goodbye to in her heart. Scott had been as dead to her as Elizabeth, their sacred marriage vow reduced to a union in name only. But like the phoenix, he had returned, transformed. And God help her, she *liked* the new Scott. Enough that even the fear of what lay ahead couldn't compel her to just walk away. She drew a shaky breath, and when she spoke her voice was slightly unsteady. "I don't mind waiting."

He studied her for a moment, and then his eyes grew soft. "Thank you," he said quietly. "I'll wrap this up as quickly as I can."

Jess watched as he made his way over to the police car, still juggling the few meager items he had salvaged. In addition to the soot on his cheek, there were now smudges on his shirt, as well. Did he have the money for new clothes? she suddenly wondered. And how would he get to the store to buy the immediate necessities? Almost no buses ran after eight o'clock at night.

More important, where was he going to sleep? From what she'd seen, he couldn't spare much money for a hotel. His sister lived in Chicago, so that wasn't a possibility. Reverend Young might be able to put him up for a couple of days, but the minister could be at the hospital—and unreachable—late into the night.

Perhaps Scott had kept in touch with some of his friends, she thought, though that seemed unlikely. Most of his ''friends'' in the years before the accident had been business associates, men who would have little loyalty to a friendship once it outlived its utility. So who was he going to call?

''All finished.''

Startled, Jess turned to find Scott once again at her window. ''That was quick.''

He shrugged. ''There wasn't much I could tell him. And I didn't lose anything of value, except some clothes.''

She nodded. ''Why don't you get in while I dig out my phone?''

Scott hesitated and glanced at his soiled hands and clothes. ''I'll get your car dirty.''

She reached down and pulled her trunk release. ''There are some rags in the back. Help yourself.''

When he joined her a few moments later, his salvaged items were neatly wrapped and tucked under one arm but he was still wiping his hands. ''This soot is insidious,'' he said ruefully.

''You've got a streak on your face, too.''

He flipped down the visor mirror, then reached up to scrub his cheek. ''Thanks.''

Jess watched him for a moment, trying to gather the courage to follow through on a plan that had been slowly taking shape in her mind. She was well aware that it flew in the face of caution—which only an hour ago had been her operative word. But somehow caution seemed less important than compassion at this point.

"Scott…"

"Mmm-hmm." He was still focused on erasing the smudge on his cheek.

"Where are you going to stay tonight?"

There was an almost imperceptible hesitation in his movement, and then he resumed rubbing. "I'm not sure yet. I'll work something out," he said lightly.

Jess drew a shaky breath, knowing that what she was about to say could change her life forever. "I—I have a spare bedroom."

His hand stilled, and slowly he turned to face her. His gaze locked with hers, intense, searching—and cautious. "Are you offering me a place to stay?" he asked carefully, as if he couldn't quite believe what he'd just heard.

She nodded jerkily, not trusting her voice.

Scott stared at Jess, momentarily speechless. Even though he believed in miracles, never in his most optimistic moments could he have envisioned an offer like this. For a long moment he gazed into the eyes that he adored, and his heart contracted with tenderness. He knew those eyes so well, knew every nuance of their expression. During their years together, he'd seen them sparkle with joy, glow with passion, shine with enthusiasm. He'd watched them flash with anger, glint with laughter, glimmer with mischief. He had learned to read her moods simply by looking into their green depths. Since his return, though, her eyes had been so guarded that he'd rarely had a clue to her feelings. But now he saw plenty of emotions. Doubt. Confusion. Caution. Fear. And most important, the glimmer of something more. Not love, certainly. Or even affection. It was more like...willingness...openness...receptivity. He couldn't quite put his finger on it. All he knew was that it represented a quantum leap forward. And suddenly his spirits soared.

Scott turned to gaze again at his ruined apartment, viewing it with new eyes. He didn't care about the contents, but the fire *had* disheartened him, and in the silence of his heart he had cried out, "What next, Lord?" The hassle of finding a new apartment, the expense of replacing his clothes when he was just getting enough cash together for a used car, the problem of emergency housing—it had all seemed overwhelming at first. And yet, in a way, the fire had been the answer to his prayer, he realized. Because by prompting Jess's offer, it had given him the opportunity to interact more closely with her and prove that while he was a new man in many ways, his love for her had never changed. Perhaps his words about the phoenix had been prophetic after all, he reflected.

Jess studied Scott's profile as he stared at the flat he had called home for the past four months. Already she was having second thoughts about her impulsive offer. Learning to forgive was one thing—but sharing her home with the man who had once shared her bed? That was rushing things. And definitely not very prudent. But how did she gracefully retract her invitation? she wondered in sudden panic, her mind racing. Should she just be honest? Say that the arrangement would probably be uncomfortable for them both, that a motel would be better for a night or two? It wouldn't set him back that much financially, she reassured herself. And it would certainly provide more peace of mind. For her, at least.

Jess was just about to voice her thoughts when Scott turned back to her, and for a moment her resolve faltered—giving him the opening he needed. Because he took one look at her face, saw the panic in her eyes and knew she was on the verge of taking back her invitation. Up until now he'd given her a chance to change her mind on every offer she'd made. But this was an opportunity he simply wasn't willing to give up—even if he had to play on her sympathy to make it stick.

"I appreciate your offer more than I can say, Jess," he said quickly, jumping in before she could speak. "I'm not sure I can reach Reverend Young tonight, and my so-called friends more or less vanished after I went to prison. I could dip into my car fund for a motel, but I hate to do that. Frankly, the bus is getting a bit old." Then he played his trump card. "But if it's too much of an inconvenience, I could always go to a homeless shelter for a few nights."

Jess's retraction died on her lips. Scott in a homeless shelter? she thought, appalled. No way! She'd be more uncomfortable thinking about him in an environment like that than coping with him in her guest room. She had to see this through. "Like…like I said, I have a spare bedroom," she said.

His smile warmed her all the way to her toes, making her feel a little better about her decision. She'd done the right thing after all, she assured herself as she put the car in gear.

She just wasn't sure it was the *safe* thing.

* * *

They made only two stops on the way home. One at a discount store so Scott could pick up a change of clothes and some toiletries. The other at a Chinese restaurant for take-out food. Nevertheless, by the time they reached her condo it was after nine.

Jess nervously hitched her purse higher on her shoulder as they approached her door. Scott was juggling both bags, so she prayed he wouldn't notice how badly her hand was shaking as she struggled to fit her key in the lock. When at last it clicked, she gave a relieved sigh and pushed open the door.

But her relief was short-lived. Because as they stepped over the threshold, the full impact of what she'd done slammed home. If she'd once been nervous because her *car* seemed too intimate, how in the world was she going to cope with living under the same roof with a man she had once loved—and who still filled her with longing?

Jess had no idea, she realized numbly as she led the way to the kitchen. But keeping her distance—both emotionally and physically—seemed like a good plan, she reasoned as she headed toward the cabinets to retrieve glasses and utensils.

"Do y-you want to clean up before we eat?" *Don't stammer,* she berated herself. *Acting nervous will only make this situation worse.* She forced herself to take a deep breath before she spoke again, and this time her voice was steadier. "I can always nuke the food if it gets cold."

"I'd like that, thanks. These clothes really absorbed that smoke smell."

She reached for a glass from the cabinet. "Okay. I'll show you where...oh!"

She watched in dismay as the glass slipped from her fingers and shattered on the tile floor. So much for not acting nervous, she thought in disgust as she bent to retrieve the shards.

"Be careful, Jess," Scott warned as he moved toward her. "Those pieces can cut like—"

"Ouch!" Jess jerked her hand back from a jagged shard. Already blood was dripping from her finger.

She heard his muttered oath as he moved beside her. "Let's get that under water." Without waiting for her to respond, he reached for her hand, drew her to her feet and led her toward the sink. He turned on the water and gently cradled her hand under the steady stream, letting her blood wash over his own hand as he leaned over to examine the cut.

Jess stared down at her delicate fingers resting in Scott's sun-browned hand and for a moment she thought her lungs were actually going to explode. So much for physical distance. Not only were they physically close, they were actually *touching*. Which was *not* good. She was losing control here, she realized. And that was scary.

Instinctively she made a move to pull her hand away. But just as instinctively Scott's grasp tightened and he turned to her, his eyes troubled.

"I'm sorry. I'm trying not to hurt you, Jess, but I need to see how deep this cut is."

Jess allowed him to put her finger back under the water. It was simpler than trying to explain that her reaction was caused by fear, not pain, she decided resignedly.

After what seemed like an eternity Scott turned off the faucet and looked down at her. "It's pretty deep, but I don't think it needs stitches. Do you have any bandages?"

She nodded. "In the bathroom. I'll get them." The words came out in a croak.

He frowned and looked at her worriedly, then took her arm and led her over to the table, where he gently pressed her into a chair. "I'll find them. Sit here until I come back. Your finger will just bleed more if you move around."

Jess didn't argue. The day's emotional overload had apparently short-circuited her brain, and she was too numb even to think. So she simply sat there until Scott reappeared with bandages and antiseptic.

"Okay, I think we're set," he said as he dropped into the chair next to her and extended his hand. "Let's have a look."

Jess gazed down at his waiting hand. The lean fingers were familiar, but the callused palm momentarily jolted her. Blue-collar hands, work roughened and sun browned, had replaced the neatly manicured, white-collar hands she remembered. Yet there was an earthy strength to them, a steadiness and sureness that hadn't been there before.

Jess's gaze flickered back to his. He was watching her, waiting patiently, but the look in his eyes disconcerted her. There was encouragement and tenderness in their depths, but also a flicker of apprehension, as if he was unsure whether she would willingly give him her hand. And, on a deeper level, her trust.

Jess hesitated for a moment, aware of the symbolism. Then, with sudden decision, she followed her heart and reached out to place her hand in his.

Scott hadn't even realized he was holding his breath until his lungs suddenly started working again. He knew Jess was second-guessing her invitation, and he'd been afraid that she would get cold feet at any moment and send him packing—until this simple gesture of trust, which reassured him that at least for tonight he was safe from eviction.

But not necessarily from temptation, he realized as he transferred his attention to her hand. His mouth went dry as he looked at the delicate fingers that had once touched him with such tenderness and love. A surge of longing swept over him, almost painful in its intensity, and it took every ounce of his willpower to remain still when what he really wanted to do was pull Jess into his arms and hold her. To feel her soft curves against the hard lines of his body. To bury his face in her fragrant hair and inhale her essence. To run his hands over her silky skin.

Scott drew a ragged breath, praying for control as he attended to the cut. Now that she knew his intentions he needed to move with extreme caution, he reminded himself. Patience, restraint and discipline were essential. He didn't want to make her even more nervous than she already was. To the point that she might very well ask him to leave. So he needed to appear calm and cool, even if he was anything but.

He cleared his throat and secured the end of the

bandage. "All done," he pronounced. "Just leave the glass on the floor and I'll clean it up in a few minutes. But I could sure use a shower first."

"I'll get you some towels," she said, rising.

He followed more slowly, taking cover behind the bag of clothing and toiletries he'd purchased.

"You can pretty much use this bath exclusively," Jess said, striving with limited success for an even tone as she placed clean towels on the counter. "I have an attached bath in my bedroom. The guest room is across the hall. I keep it ready, because Mark visits occasionally when he's passing through town. If you need anything, let me know. I'll be in the kitchen when you're finished." And with that rush of words, she made a fast exit.

Scott took a long, cold shower, and by the time he returned to the kitchen Jess had cleaned up the floor. He thought about saying something, but decided to let it pass. "The food smells great," he pronounced.

At the sound of his voice, the pulse rate Jess had just gotten under control once again accelerated. And when she turned from the sink, it slammed into high gear. Scott was standing in the doorway, and he looked...*fabulous* was the word that came to mind. His damp hair was slicked back, and though his clothes might not be designer brands, they fit as if custom made. The jeans hugged his slim hips and outlined his long muscular legs, and his black T-shirt revealed impressive biceps. Jess nodded jerkily toward the table, where she'd set two places. "I reheated everything," she said a bit breathlessly. "Have a seat."

"Can I help with anything?"

Her eyebrows rose in surprise. That wasn't an offer she was used to hearing. Even in the early days of their marriage Scott hadn't been into housekeeping-type duties. He'd taken care of the outdoor chores, leaving indoor jobs to her. "No. Everything's ready. What would you like to drink?"

He glanced at the glasses of water on the table. "This is fine."

Jess scooped the food onto platters, then joined him at the table. He eyed it hungrily and smiled. "I haven't had any really good Chinese food in a long time," he said, reaching for a serving spoon.

"Even since…in the few months?"

He shook his head. "I usually eat in."

Because it was cheaper. The words were left unsaid, but Jess could read between the lines. "Well, I think you'll like this. I found this place shortly after I moved in here, and I go so often we're on a first-name basis now."

Scott ate as if he hadn't seen food in a week, clearly savoring every bite. "You don't cook anymore?"

"Not much."

"I thought you enjoyed it."

"I did. Once upon a time. But cooking for one isn't much fun. I just…got out of the habit."

They ate in silence for a few moments, then Scott gestured toward his surroundings. "I like the condo. And you've done a nice job decorating it."

"Thanks."

It was a perfunctory reply to what she clearly considered to be a perfunctory compliment, so Scott tried again. "I mean it, Jess. It's comfortable and homey, but not cluttered. I like the clean lines and colors."

She looked at him in surprise, and this time her tone was warmer. "Thank you. Actually, I haven't devoted too much attention to the place. I just wanted something simple and uncomplicated to come home to at the end of the day."

"A haven from a world that usually isn't either of those things," he said quietly.

She gave him a thoughtful look, struck by his insight. "I hadn't thought of it that way," she said slowly. "But you're probably right."

"Simple is good," he reflected. "That's why I wasn't very upset by the fire. Almost everything is replaceable. And I salvaged the things I really wanted. The horticulture books were given to me by Karen and Reverend Young, so they have sentimental—and practical—value. The cross was made by a former inmate who became a good friend. He sent it to me a few months ago, after he got out. And the picture—well, that's been with me ever since I...since the accident. I'll clean it all up later."

She nodded. "I put everything in the laundry room. And feel free to use the washer and dryer."

"Thanks. I'd also like to call Karen to let her know where I am, if that's okay. She can ring me right back so we don't run up your bill."

She waved his offer aside. "Don't worry about it."

"Thanks." Scott scraped up the last bite of chicken broccoli and then gave a sigh of satisfaction. "That was great." He nodded toward her plate, well aware that she'd spent more time pushing her food around than eating, which probably explained why she was so thin. "Are you finished?"

"Yes."

He reached for her plate and stood. "I'll take care of the dishes." At her astonished look, he chuckled. "I told you I've changed," he reminded her with a wink. Then he glanced at his watch and gave a low whistle. "Hey, this is way past your bedtime! Why don't you turn in? You're going to have trouble getting in your eight hours tonight as it is."

Which was nothing new, she thought. Five or six hours were about the most she could manage these days. But she let the comment pass. "All right. Thanks. See you in the morning."

She got as far as the door before his voice stopped her.

"Jess."

She paused and slowly turned. Though they were several feet apart, she could feel the warmth in his gaze as if it was a caress.

"Thank you again for doing this," he said quietly.

"You're welcome," she whispered. And then she fled.

"Karen? Sorry to call you so late."

"Scott? What's wrong?"

"Nothing. I'm fine. Relax," he hastened to reassure her. "I'm at a different phone number for the next couple of nights, and I just wanted to give it to you in case you need to reach me for any reason."

"Why are you at a different number?"

"Just take it down, then call me back and I'll answer all your questions.'' He gave her the number, then hung up. When the phone rang a moment later, he snatched it up immediately so Jess wouldn't be disturbed.

''Okay, what gives?'' Karen demanded without preamble.

''There was a fire at my flat, and—''

''Are you hurt?'' she asked in alarm.

''No. I'm fine. I just need to find a new place to stay.''

''What happened at the flat?''

''Faulty wiring.''

He heard her unladylike snort across the wire. ''Why am I not surprised? Well, as far as I'm concerned, good riddance. That place was a dive.''

''Oh, come on. Don't hold back. Tell me how you really feel,'' he teased her.

''Ha ha. So where are you staying?''

''Jess's condo.''

For once, his sister was struck dumb. At least for a moment. ''Do you want to explain that?'' she asked when she finally found her voice.

He chuckled. ''I thought you'd be surprised.''

''That, my dear brother, is a gross understatement.''

''Remember the retreat I told you about, the one where I was going to speak?''

''Yes. It was today. I was going to call you tomorrow and see how it went.''

''It went fine. No surprises. Except one. Jess was there.''

''You're kidding! You never told me she was coming!''

"Because I didn't know. Anyway, I don't think she planned to tell *me*, either, but as she was leaving she happened to overhear Reverend Young and me talking. The guy who was supposed to give me a ride got sick, so she stepped in and offered to take me home."

"You're kidding!"

"You said that already. And no, I'm not."

"Well, go on," she said impatiently. "How did you end up at her condo?"

"When we got to the flat, there were emergency vehicles all over. The building had been evacuated, and she offered me her guest room."

"Wow!" Karen breathed in awe.

"Yeah, wow."

"You know, this is all too much to be coincidence," she said thoughtfully.

"That thought did cross my mind."

"It looks like your prayers are being answered. Make that *our* prayers."

"Looks that way. But do me a favor, okay?"

"Sure."

"Keep praying. Because now that I have my foot in the door, literally and figuratively, one wrong move could blow the whole thing."

"Keep the faith, Scott. I don't think the Lord would have brought you this far to slam the door in your face."

"I hope not. But one thing I've learned, Karen. Never take anything for granted. And always be prepared for the unexpected."

Chapter Ten

Jess turned to squint at the illuminated dial of her bedside clock and groaned. Two-thirty. In four hours she'd have to get up. And so far she'd had virtually no sleep.

Restlessly she turned on her side and scrunched her pillow under her head. She hadn't heard a sound out of Scott since she'd closed her door for the night, so she couldn't blame her sleeplessness on a noisy house guest. No, it was the house guest *himself* who was keeping her awake. If she didn't sleep all that well on a *typical* night, she might as well throw in the towel tonight, which was about as far from typical as they came, she thought wryly.

With a resigned sigh, Jess swung her legs to the floor and stood, hitching up the shoulder on her oversize T-shirt as she stretched wearily. Maybe a cup of herbal tea would help her doze, she thought hopefully. Four hours of rest wasn't enough, but it would be better than nothing.

Jess moved to her door and cracked it slightly, listening intently. Silence. She glanced at the guest-room door. Closed. Scott was obviously asleep. Lucky him, she thought enviously as she opened her door and padded quietly down the hall.

Normally she made her tea the old-fashioned way, in a kettle, but tonight she settled for the faster and quieter microwave. As she waited for the water to boil, she glanced around the spotless kitchen. True to his word, Scott had washed their dinner dishes. She peeked into the laundry room. His personal items were gone, so apparently he'd cleaned up those, too.

Jess removed her mug from the microwave and dipped her tea bag in the hot water, mulling over all that had happened in the past eight hours. If anyone had told her this morning that Scott would be spending the night at her condo, she would have laughed in their face. And yet here he was, sleeping only a few feet away.

Jess drew a shaky breath and wandered into the living room, stopping in front of the photo of Elizabeth. It was slightly out of position, and as she reached for it she suddenly knew that Scott had also held it in his hands tonight. What had gone through his mind? she wondered with a bittersweet pang as she sank into an overstuffed chair and tucked her feet under her. Had he thought about all that might have been, as she so often had? Of the two of them watching their daughter grow? Of brothers and sisters joining the family? Of school plays and piano lessons and soccer games? Of first dates and graduations and, eventually, weddings? Of stolen romantic moments that kept the love be-

tween the two of them young and vibrant? Of grand-
children, who would add sunshine and youth to their
days as they grew old together? And in the end, of
looking back on a long life together and finding con-
tentment and satisfaction in the circle of love they had
created that would go on long after they had departed
this earth? Had he thought of all those things? she
wondered. And if so, had his stomach knotted painfully—as hers always did—making him feel physically sick to know that they would never be?

Suddenly Jess realized that tears were streaming
down her face, and she reached up to wipe them away,
hugging Elizabeth's picture to her chest. She set the
mug down, then let her head drop back on the chair,
struggling to control the feeling of bleakness and desolation that always swept over her when she allowed
herself to think about the "what ifs." It wasn't a
healthy thing to do. She knew that from counseling,
so she rarely indulged herself. But the emotional
events of today, the fact that the man who had destroyed her dreams was sleeping a mere few feet away,
made it impossible not to think about what might have
been. And to wish, vain though it was, that they could
go back in time and start over.

Jess closed her eyes wearily. Scott seemed intent on
making a fresh start. Seemed to believe that it was
possible to begin again. But she wasn't as optimistic.
They had too much baggage. The hate she'd felt for
four years wouldn't turn into love overnight, even if
she *was* impressed by the changes in him. Even if she
had, in fact, grown to like this new Scott. Nor could
she seem to get rid of her own guilt, the thought that

if she'd insisted on driving the night of the accident things might have turned out differently. The one thing they did have going for them, she admitted, was chemistry. Amazingly, that was just as powerful as it had always been. But it wasn't enough to sustain a relationship over the long term. The baggage had to be dealt with, too.

Mark had told her that seeing Scott might help her do that. So she was making an effort. Like going to the retreat today. And hearing Scott talk candidly about his mistakes, his regrets and his hopes *had* helped. She understood for the first time—maybe *let* herself understand for the first time—the pain and desolation he had suffered, which had been no less than hers. And—even harder to admit—perhaps worse. Because *he* was the *cause* of hers. Scott had never been a man who wanted to cause anyone pain, least of all his family. That's why he'd struggled so hard trying to juggle the often conflicting demands of his job and his family. Why he'd seemed so often frustrated. Why he'd turned to alcohol to ease the stress.

And for that, too, Jess felt guilt, she acknowledged. Perhaps if she had been more understanding they wouldn't have begun to drift apart. Perhaps he wouldn't have needed the alcohol. Perhaps the accident would never have happened.

Once more tears trickled out of the corners of her eyes. And this time she made no attempt to wipe them away. Mark was very likely right when he'd suggested that she had simply buried her issues instead of dealing with them. But doing so had allowed her to cope, to go on living what *appeared* to be a normal life. Even if that life was a pretense, it had given her something to cling to, allowed her to stay afloat.

But now she was adrift—and sinking fast.

Scott opened his eyes, instantly awake, his heart racing. He stared at the dark ceiling, momentarily disoriented, and tensed, suddenly on guard—a reflex born of an environment where being ready for anything was the only way to survive. But then the events of the preceding day came rushing back, and his coiled muscles slowly relaxed. He was in Jess's condo. And it wasn't just a dream.

For several moments Scott lay quietly, savoring the feeling of freedom, of safety and, most of all, of proximity to the woman he loved. She was just a few feet away, he thought in wonder, swallowing past the lump that suddenly appeared in his throat. So many times in prison, when he'd awakened in the middle of the night overcome by a crushing sensation of desperate loneliness, he'd closed his eyes and forced himself to pretend that he wasn't really alone. That Jess was nearby.

And now she was.

Impulsively he swung his feet to the floor, closing the distance to the hall in three long strides. It might be silly, but he just wanted to look at her room. To stare at her door and imagine her sleeping just on the other side, curled on her side, her hair spilling over her pillow, her chin tucked into her shoulder in the endearing sleep position she favored. Often he'd awakened and found her in that pose. And sometimes, in the early days of their marriage, he'd been so over-

come by gratitude for the gift of her love that a rush
of tenderness would sweep over him as he watched
her sleep, so strong it brought tears to his eyes. But
as the demands of his job increasingly sapped his energy and attention, he'd become too preoccupied to
notice such things. Or appreciate them.

Those days were over, however. Never again would
he take such blessings for granted, he vowed.

Scott quietly opened his door and looked down the
hall, frowning when he realized that Jess's door was
wide open and her bed empty. He glanced over his
shoulder at the illuminated dial of the bedside clock.
Three in the morning. She had always been a sound
sleeper. What was wrong? Was her finger hurting?
Had it started to bleed again? The cut had been deep—
maybe she should have had stitches, he thought worriedly.

Scott eased his door shut and strode toward the chair
where he'd draped his clothes, reaching for his jeans
and stepping into them in one rapid, fluid motion.
Then he returned to the hall, pulling on his T-shirt as
he walked, and quietly made his way to the kitchen,
only to find the room dark—and deserted. His frown
deepened, and he turned to the living room, which was
faintly illuminated by a low-watt lamp. And that's
where he found her.

She was curled in an overstuffed chair, a half-empty
mug on the floor beside her, a framed photo pressed
against her chest. And judging by her even breathing,
she was asleep. Slowly he moved closer, until he stood
directly above her. Though the light was dim, he could
see the evidence of tears on her pale cheeks, the dark

shadows under her eyes, the troubled frown on her face that even sleep didn't erase. His gut clenched painfully and he drew a ragged breath. She looked so fragile. So vulnerable. So alone.

Scott thought about the Jess he had known in happier days—strong, vibrant, in love with life. Certainly the strength was still there. She couldn't have survived these past few years if it hadn't been. But she'd paid a price for her survival. There was an unnatural tension about her, a nervous energy that spoke of long-term stress. She now seemed more focused on making it through the day than on *enjoying* the day. And her vibrant personality was now subdued, her joy replaced by a deep, abiding sadness that whispered even at the edges of her infrequent smiles.

Hardest of all to bear was the knowledge that he was the cause of her distress. And his heart wept yet again for the havoc his misguided priorities and tragic lapse in judgment had wreaked on the woman he loved more than life itself.

Suddenly Jess's eyelids flickered open, and she looked up at him sleepily, momentarily confused. "Scott?"

For a second he was disconcerted by her unexpected awakening. But he recovered quickly, forcing his lips into a smile as he squatted beside her. "Bingo. What are you doing out here in the middle of the night?" he asked unevenly, his eyes only inches from hers.

Her vision suddenly cleared as the last vestiges of sleep vanished, and she straightened up abruptly. Her rapid movement caused the neckline of her T-shirt to slip and the hem to creep up, giving Scott a quick glimpse of a creamy shoulder and a long length of shapely thigh. She gasped and made a frantic grab for both ends of the garment, dropping the picture in the process.

Scott bent to retrieve it, struggling to control the surge of longing that left him suddenly way too warm. She, on the other hand, seemed cold—or, more likely, nervous—he noted when he turned back to her. She was visibly trembling, one hand clutching the neckline of her T-shirt, the other pulling the hem as far down as it would go. He set the photo back on the coffee table and headed across the room toward the couch to retrieve a throw, which he silently draped over her—for both their sakes.

She snuggled under it gratefully, covering every possible bit of exposed skin. Only then did she look up at him, and when she did her mouth went dry. How could a man with uncombed hair and stubble on his face look so appealing? she marveled. With an effort she tore her gaze from his face and let it drop lower. He wore the same T-shirt he'd had on at dinner, she noted, and his jeans had obviously been hastily pulled on, sans belt. He hadn't even bothered with socks or shoes, she realized, staring at his bare feet far too long before she found her voice. "Th-thank you."

"My pleasure." The rough, whiskeylike quality in his voice drew her gaze back to his. "So what are you doing up at this hour?"

"I—I couldn't sleep."

He sat on the ottoman in front of her and rested his forearms on his knees, clasping his hands in front of him. "Something you ate?"

She shifted uncomfortably. "No. I—I just don't sleep very well anymore."

He frowned. "Since when?"

"For a while," she hedged.

"Since when, Jess?" he persisted, gazing at her intently.

She sighed. Why hide it? "Since the accident."

He let his breath out slowly. "Almost four years," he said quietly. "No wonder you always look so tired. How much sleep do you get?"

"I don't know. Five, maybe six hours a night."

He glanced at his watch. "Or less." He looked at her worriedly. "That's not enough."

"It's as much as you ever got."

"I don't need as much sleep as most people."

"Even so...why are *you* up? Three o'clock is late even for you."

He raked his fingers through his hair. "I don't know. Strange place. Strange noises. I'm a pretty light sleeper now."

She looked at him curiously. "That's a switch. You may not have needed *much* sleep, but when you did sleep it took practically an earthquake to wake you."

At the intimate reference, his lips quirked briefly into a smile, but when he spoke his voice was sober. "Prison does strange things to you. You learn to be on alert pretty much all the time."

"Why?"

He looked at her silently for a minute. "Let's just say that it's not a very nice place, Jess. Or a safe one," he said quietly.

She stared at him, suddenly feeling sick. As open

as he'd been in his talk at the retreat, there were obviously a lot of things he hadn't revealed. Bad things.

"I'm sorry," she whispered.

"Hey, I survived," he said reassuringly. "It's over. And good came out of the experience, for which I'm grateful. Now it's just a matter of putting the bad behind me."

She gazed at him, and the wistful look in her eyes tugged at his heart. "How will you do that?"

He drew a deep breath. "By focusing on the good," he replied simply. "One thing I learned, Jess. You can't forget the past. God knows, I tried. I'd still like to erase the memory of the bad days in our marriage, of the accident, of the trial, of prison. But I can't. It's part of me, both the good and bad. And that's true for everyone. So eventually you have to accept the past, learn what you can from it, then leave it behind and move on."

"That's not an easy thing to do," she whispered.

Without even thinking, he reached over and took her hand, cradling it between his. In the quiet of the night he heard her sharply indrawn breath, but she didn't pull away. "I know," he said hoarsely. "Dear God, I know!" He glanced toward the picture of Elizabeth, and when he spoke his voice was choked with emotion. "I used to lie awake wondering what she would have been like as she grew up. Would she have liked soccer? Gymnastics? Chess? Would she have taken ballet lessons? Would she have been good at math? I even tried to imagine the holidays and the birthday parties and the proms we'll never share with her." He drew a ragged breath, clearly struggling for control. "Sometimes I still think about all that. But mostly I try to think of the joy she brought to my life. Of her enthusiasm and her infectious smile and the way she could make me feel warm inside, and important, with just a look. She gave me so many gifts in her short life, Jess. I can't bring her back, but neither can anyone take away those gifts. That's what I try to remember."

When he looked back at Jess, tears were once more streaming down her face. He reached over and gently brushed them away, blinking back his own. "I'm sorry," he whispered brokenly, his eyes anguished. "Dear God, I'm so sorry for all the pain I caused you!"

Jess looked down at their entwined hands. The impulse to reach for him, to let him take her in his arms and hold her until the world went away with all its grief and guilt and regrets, was so strong that it frightened her. Her need for comfort was always most intense in the quiet, dark, early-morning hours when she invariably felt most alone, and the temptation to simply follow her impulses was powerful. But in the light of day she would most likely regret such a rash action, she cautioned herself. It was too soon. And even though she believed that Scott's remorse was genuine, it couldn't restore the life she had known.

Carefully she disengaged her hand from his, struggling to ignore the disappointment in his eyes. "I'm working on forgiveness, Scott," she told him. "But I—I can't make any promises."

"I'm not asking you to. I'm just asking you not to shut me out. To give me a chance."

She sighed. "I don't seem to have a lot of choice in the matter, considering how life seems to be throwing us together."

"Maybe that's a sign." The soft chime of a clock sounded in the darkness, and Scott glanced at his watch, angling toward the light that barely illuminated the room. "Three-thirty! You need to get some sleep."

"What about you?"

Sleep was the last thing on his mind. "I think I'll have some coffee first."

"All right. There's instant decaf in the cabinet by the stove." She wrapped the throw more tightly around her and stood. "I'll see you tomorrow."

And as she disappeared down the hall he let her parting comment echo in his mind, savoring the most wonderful words he'd heard in a long, long time.

"Here you are, sir." Scott handed the customer his change, and the man folded the money together with the rest of his cash before shoving the roll of bills into his pocket. "Now let me help you get everything to your car."

Scott moved to the other side of the counter and reached for the two trays of annuals while the man picked up a hanging basket of fuchsia.

"Looks like you're going to have a nice garden," Scott commented as they made their way across the parking lot.

"My wife used to do all the gardening, but her arthritis has slowed her down considerably. So now she supervises and I plant,'' he said good-naturedly. ''But I don't have her green thumb.''

''Well, impatiens and begonias are pretty forgiving, so they were good choices,'' Scott said as the man opened his trunk and placed his plants inside. ''You should be fine.''

''Thanks again for your help.''

''My pleasure.''

Scott turned and headed back toward the main building, only to pull up abruptly a few feet from the car when his gaze came to rest on a stack of folded bills that looked suspiciously like the ones the customer had just shoved into his pocket. Scott bent and picked up the money, flipping through it. There was more than two hundred dollars in the roll, he realized, recalling the days when that amount of money was just pocket change to him. Now it was a fortune. And it would certainly beef up his car fund—if he was the kind of man to be swayed by such temptation. But it just wasn't in his nature. He turned back to the car, flagging the customer down as he pulled out of the parking spot.

''I think you dropped this, sir,'' he said, handing the roll of bills through the window.

The man frowned and reached into his pocket. ''Good heavens! You're right. Thank you so much!'' he said gratefully as he took the money. ''I guess there are still some honest people around after all.''

Scott grinned and stepped back. ''A few. Enjoy the flowers.''

''I will. And thanks again.''

Scott watched the man drive away, then turned back

toward the main building—only to find Seth watching the scenario from a few feet away, fists on his hips, chomping on his ever-present unlit cigar. For a moment Scott's step faltered. Though the nursery owner never said much, Scott had developed great respect for him as a businessman—and a person. Seth had not only given him a chance when few were willing to take on an ex-con, but had steadily increased Scott's responsibility. After Scott's first design project went well, Seth had moved him permanently into the retail side of the business and funneled more such projects his way. He'd also given him a nice bump in salary. So even though Seth didn't offer much verbal praise, his actions spoke loud and clear. But right now Scott wasn't quite sure how to read the enigmatic look on the man's face. And he certainly wasn't expecting the man's first words.

"I think I found you a car."

Scott stared at him, his expression momentarily blank. "A car?"

Seth gave a quick nod. "I have a friend who's a mechanic. I asked him to keep an eye out for you. He thinks he's got a good one." Seth gave Scott the particulars, including the attractive price. "You can trust Les. He's a good man. I told him you might stop by on your lunch hour to take a look."

"I'd like to," Scott said with a frown. "But I'm already short on hours today." His work day had started with an apology to Seth for his late arrival because of the unfamiliar bus schedule from Jess's condo.

Seth waved his comment aside. "You work harder

in eight hours than most people do in twelve. Don't worry about it. I have to run an errand at lunch time, so I can drop you off at his shop and pick you up on my way back."

Scott hardly knew what to say. So he settled for a simple but heartfelt "Thank you."

"Meet me in the office at eleven-thirty," Seth said gruffly, turning toward the main building. As Scott watched the nursery owner stride away, his throat tightened in gratitude. Reverend Young had been right about Seth. The man might not practice much formal religion, but he lived the Christian values more fully than many churchgoing people Scott had met. Though Scott had been warned to expect the stigma of his prison record to follow him, it had still been a shock to experience reactions ranging from caution to distrust to aversion when people found out he was an ex-con. Even people at church. Some had been wonderful, of course, accepting him fully and welcoming him into their midst. But in the eyes of others he'd seen judgment and condemnation, as if his mistakes had tainted him forever. Those were rough moments. Discouraging moments. But thank God there were good people, too. Like Seth. And Reverend Young. People who believed in him and were willing to give him a chance.

Now, if only he could convince Jess to do the same.

The doorbell interrupted Scott's perusal of the real estate listings, and he set the paper aside with a discouraged sigh. Finding a reasonably priced apartment was proving difficult—especially since he'd promised

Karen he would upgrade his previous lodgings. But he'd have his car tomorrow, and then he could check out a few places in person—which should expedite things, he thought as he walked toward the door.

Fortunately, after seeing the long hours he worked and the time it took to travel by bus, Jess had told him that she didn't mind if it took him a few days to find a place to stay. He didn't intend to take advantage of her generosity, of course—but neither did he plan to rush. This time with her was a blessing, and he didn't want the opportunity to see her on a daily basis to end any sooner than necessary. It was too close to heaven, he thought, his lips curving into a smile.

The smile was still on his face when he opened the door a moment later, but it froze when he came face-to-face with Jess's parents. Their own smiles quickly gave way to shock, and from there her father's expression degenerated to hostility.

"What are you doing here?" Frank asked curtly, his face growing ruddy.

Scott's stomach twisted into a knot. "Hello, Frank. Clare. There was a fire at my flat, and Jess offered me her guest room until I found a new apartment."

"Where is she?"

"On her way home, I suspect. She should be here any minute. Would you like to come in and wait?"

"No, we would not."

"Is there anything I can help you with?"

"Yes. You can leave Jess alone!" Frank said furiously.

Scott felt a hot flush creep up his neck, and he struggled to maintain a cordial tone when he spoke. "I think that's between me and Jess."

Frank's face grew redder. "Really? Well, I don't. Not after what you did to her. Not after you left her mother and me to pick up the pieces. Good God, man, don't you think you've done enough damage? Do you have any idea how long it took her to get back on her feet after the accident? To be able to make it through a day without shaking so badly that she had to take medication? Do you know how many months she spent in counseling? And now you waltz back into her life and turn it upside down all over again! Don't think her mother and I haven't noticed the changes in her since you came back, either. Or that we haven't spent sleepless nights worrying that she'll end up on the verge of a nervous breakdown again. If you cared for her at all, you'd leave her alone. You'd walk out of her life and never come back."

By the time Frank finished his furious tirade, Scott felt almost physically sick. He had known just by looking at her that the past few years had taken an immense toll on Jess. But apparently the trauma had been even worse than he'd imagined. He'd had no idea she'd come that close to a nervous breakdown. Was Frank right? he wondered. Had his return caused more harm than good? Would Jess be better off without him?

With a weary sigh Scott raked his fingers through his hair and gazed at Jess's parents. "The last thing in the world I want to do is hurt Jess again," he said with quiet sincerity, his eyes troubled. "I love her. I always have and I always will. I realize I've made some bad mistakes. And I spent three long, lonely years in prison thinking about them. But the one thing that wasn't a mistake was marrying Jess. She's always been the best part of my life. It may have taken a tragedy for me to realize that, but now that I have, I want to spend the rest of *my* life filling *hers* with joy. I just don't see how that could be bad for her. Or for us.''

There was silence for a moment while the two men stared at each other. Then Frank turned away. "Come on, Clare. Let's get out of here," he said coldly.

Scott transferred his gaze to Jess's mother, whose eyes were far less hostile than her husband's. She looked at him for a long moment, then held out a foil-covered dish. "I was going to drop this off for Jess," she said softly. "She likes my pot roast, and we had extra. There's enough for two."

Gratitude filled Scott's eyes as he reached for the container. "Thank you."

She nodded, then turned and joined her husband, who had moved a few feet away. He took her arm stiffly, and without a backward glance they walked away.

Slowly Scott closed the door and tiredly made his way to the kitchen, feeling suddenly drained. He slipped the casserole dish into the oven, then sank into one of the kitchen chairs and let his head drop into his hands. For the first time since his release he was actually tempted to have a beer. Working outdoors in the heat and humidity of the St. Louis summer had taken its toll physically, and the encounter with Jess's parents had taken its toll mentally. Yeah, a beer would taste good about now, he thought. Except he didn't drink anymore. Not even beer. He'd had enough trouble with alcohol to last ten lifetimes.

The phone rang, and Scott automatically reached for it. "Hello."

There was silence for a moment, and Scott frowned. He wasn't in the mood for games. Or for recorded phone solicitations, he thought irritably. He was just about to hang up when a voice on the other end spoke.

"Scott?"

Scott's irritation changed to puzzlement. No one knew he was here, except Seth and Karen. And this voice belonged to neither. "Yes?" he replied cautiously.

"I thought it was you. Sorry. It just took me by surprise. This is Mark."

Scott closed his eyes and groaned silently. Great. Just what he needed. A browbeating by yet another member of Jess's family. "Hello, Mark," he said coolly.

"So Jess finally took my advice, I see."

Scott's frown reappeared. "What are you talking about?"

Mark chuckled. "I can see she didn't give her brother credit for his brilliant counsel. By the way, welcome back."

At Mark's friendly tone, the tension in Scott's shoulders eased. As did his frown. "Thanks. What advice?"

"When she told me you were out and trying to talk to her, I told her to listen. She's kept everything bottled up inside for too long. And while *she* may think she's dealt with her issues and moved on, *I* know better. You guys had a good thing going for a long time. Frankly, I think you still do. The trick is convincing her.''

Scott felt the last vestiges of tension vanish, and he expelled a relieved sigh. ''Thanks.''

''For what?''

''For not hating me. For trying to convince Jess to give me a chance. For calling when you did—right after I opened the door and gave your parents the shock of their lives.''

''Ouch. I take it they didn't know you two have been talking?''

''They might have. But they didn't know I was staying here.''

There was silence for a moment, and when Mark spoke his voice was cautious. ''You want to explain that?''

Scott smiled. ''It's not what you think. Unfortunately. There was a fire at my flat a couple of days ago, and Jess offered me her spare bedroom.''

''No kidding! So how are things going?''

''I'm still here.''

''Yeah. Good point. I'd call that progress,'' Mark said encouragingly. ''Is she around?''

''Not yet. She should be here any minute.''

''Okay. I'll get back with her later. In the meantime, hang in there. I have a good feeling about this. I know my sister. Even when she thought she hated you, she didn't. She just hated what you *did*. In fact, I'd go so far as to say that she still loves you. But hey, enough of this mushy stuff. I gotta run. If you need to hear a friendly voice, though, just give me a ring. Anytime.''

The line went dead, and slowly Scott replaced the receiver, his expression thoughtful. Could Mark be right? he wondered. Did Jess still love him?

He wasn't as sure about that as Mark. But he did agree that her invitation to stay was definitely progress. And for right now, that was good enough.

Chapter Eleven

Scott had been listening for Jess, and when he heard her key in the lock he rose and headed for the foyer. He wasn't looking forward to telling her about her parents' visit, but he would rather she heard about it from him first.

"Someone's been cooking," she said with a surprised look, sniffing appreciatively as she leaned down to deposit her briefcase and purse on the floor. "It kind of smells like my mom's pot roast."

Scott took a deep breath. "It is."

Jess froze for a second, then slowly rose and turned to him in dismay.

"She and your dad stopped by a little while ago to drop it off."

Jess reached up to tuck her hair behind her ear, her eyes troubled. "I'm sure that wasn't very pleasant for you."

He shrugged. "I survived. Frankly, I'm more worried about *you.*"

"Don't be. I can handle it."

She was putting up a good front, he acknowledged, but her voice lacked conviction and she was clearly agitated. He watched as she moved into the living room and stopped to stare unseeingly out the window, one hand on her hip, the other massaging her temple.

"It's my own fault for waiting to tell them," she said with a sigh. "I was going to break the news when I went to their house for dinner on Thursday, hoping that in a relaxed atmosphere they might be a bit more receptive. But that was just wishful thinking. They have strong feelings on the subject. Especially Dad." She turned to Scott with a frown. "What did they say?"

"Your mother was pleasant enough," he hedged.

"Which means Dad wasn't," she said flatly, dropping onto the couch. "Why am I not surprised?" Wearily she passed a hand over her eyes. "Nothing's ever easy, is it?"

Scott watched her silently, read her inner struggle in her eyes. It wasn't fair to make her choose between him and her parents. He didn't have the right to impose that burden on her. Much as he wanted to extend his stay, he couldn't do so if it made life more difficult for her. He jammed his hands into his pockets and took a deep breath. "I don't want to cause you any more problems, Jess. I can be out of here in an hour."

She frowned. "Did you find an apartment?"

"Not yet. But it's only a matter of days."

Slowly she shook her head, and her chin tilted up ever so slightly. "No. I offered you a place to stay, and I'm not backing down. It's my decision, not theirs," she said defiantly. "As much as I love Mom and Dad, they're wrong about this. It's my life. I have to live it as I think best, whether they agree or not." She rose and strode toward the door, pausing only to reach for her purse. "I'll be back in a little while. It's time Mom and Dad and I talked this thing out."

It had not gone well, Jess thought despondently as she got into her car. Actually, "abysmal" might be a better way to describe the encounter with her parents. Although her mother had been somewhat receptive, her father had stubbornly refused to listen to anything that conflicted with his firmly entrenched opinions, summarily dismissing the notion that Scott might truly have repented and changed. When their "discussion" degenerated to the point of becoming a shouting match, Jess had simply walked out.

She drove aimlessly for a time, too upset to return to the condo and face Scott but with no other destination in mind—until she suddenly thought about the meditation garden he'd designed for his church. She'd made a point to note the name of the church on his drawing, thinking that she might stop by sometime to see in person what she had so admired on paper. And suddenly this seemed as good a time as any. A contemplative, quiet place to think was just what she needed.

When Jess pulled into the deserted parking lot a few minutes later, dusk was starting to descend. A slight breeze gently stirred the warm air, giving the illusion of coolness, and the birds were just beginning their twilight song. She made her way toward the back of the church, pausing in admiration when she turned the corner. The rough pencil sketch had hardly done justice to the garden Scott had designed, she realized as her appreciative gaze swept over the scene.

A natural-wood gazebo stood gracefully on a small rise and was reflected in the surface of the placid lake beside it. A curving path led to the structure, weaving in and out among banks of glorious flowers that spilled down in welcoming array. As Jess slowly made her way toward the lake, she felt enveloped in color and harmony—the result of expert design, she realized. And by the time she stepped into the gazebo, her tension had eased considerably.

Jess sank onto the wooden bench that rimmed the inside of the structure and thought about the creator of this oasis of peace and harmony and tranquillity. Her husband. The man she had once loved with a passion that had seemed destined to endure for all time. But in the end, it hadn't been strong enough to survive hardship and tragedy. Oh, the passion had been. No question about that. But the love...that was different. Love was so much more than just hormones. It was trust and consideration and respect and communication and sharing and commitment. It was putting the other person's needs above your own. It was supporting them and believing in them even when the world didn't.

And it was forgiving.

Jess drew a long, shaky breath. The Scott who had emerged from the gray walls of prison was a man who, under other circumstances, she could easily fall in love with, she acknowledged. But they weren't beginning a relationship from scratch. They had a history together, one filled with pain and loss and tragedy. And so their future very much depended on forgiveness. Hers.

"Jess?"

She turned, startled. "Reverend Young!"

The minister closed the distance between them, pausing at the edge of the gazebo. "I'm sorry. Am I disturbing you?"

She managed a wry smile. "Relatively speaking, no."

"May I join you, then?"

"Of course."

He stepped up into the gazebo and sat across from her, gazing out over the lake. "This is a great spot, isn't it? I usually come back here for a few minutes to refresh my soul whenever I stop by the church. Scott did a great job." He paused for a moment to savor the view, then turned back to her. "By the way, I spoke with him a little while ago," he said. At her surprised look, he smiled. "We stay in close touch. I told him when he got out that I would always be available as a sounding board, and I'm happy to say he takes me up on the offer regularly. He told me about his encounter with your parents. And that you had gone to talk with them. I'm sure that wasn't easy."

Jess sighed. "No." Now it was her turn to gaze out over the lake. "They're having a hard time understanding why I've let Scott back into my life. And frankly, so am I. I've hated him for four years, and yet I invite him to stay at my condo." She shook her head, bewildered. "It doesn't make any sense."

"It might," Reverend Young said mildly.

Jess turned to him with a frown. "What do you mean?"

"Well, it all depends on whether the Scott you invited to stay at your condo is the same Scott who went to prison."

She looked at him thoughtfully. "In some ways, yes," she said slowly. "But he's changed quite a bit, too. For the better."

"Then maybe your invitation does make sense."

"Tell that to my parents," she said with a sigh.

"What do *they* think you should do?"

"Tell him to get lost. They still hate him for what he did to Elizabeth—and to me."

"And what about you, Jess? How do you feel about him?" he asked gently.

"I don't know." She rose restlessly and moved closer to the lake side of the gazebo, pressing her palms flat on the railing as she stared out over the water. "I used to hate him. But I'm tired of hating. And I—I'm not sure anymore that everything I blamed on him was all his fault, anyway." She paused, trying to gather the courage to speak what had long been in her heart. "The thing is, I shouldn't have *let* him drive that night," she said slowly. "If I'd been behind the wheel, maybe Elizabeth and the judge wouldn't have been killed. And if I'd been more understanding about his pressures at work, maybe he wouldn't have turned to alcohol in the first place."

She was afraid that when she turned she would see censure and recrimination in the minister's eyes. Instead, they reflected kindness and compassion.

"Guilt can be a terrible burden," he said quietly. "It can rob our lives of joy and hope and peace. We all do the best we can under the circumstances in which we find ourselves. Sometimes we make good choices. Sometimes we don't. That's part of being human. And we can't spend our lives beating ourselves up over the bad choices. At some point we have to accept the mistakes we've made, forgive ourselves and move on."

"You sound like Scott." She forced her lips into the semblance of a smile. "Or maybe he sounds like you."

Reverend Young chuckled. "The concept may have started with me—or, more accurately, with the Lord," he admitted. "But Scott took it to heart, though he'll be the first to admit that he struggled mightily with it. Sometimes it's easier to forgive others than to forgive ourselves, you know. But in the end, he felt the healing power of God."

Jess looked at him wistfully. "I wish I could."

"You can. You just have to ask for forgiveness— and most important, be willing to follow His example by forgiving others."

She drew a deep breath. "Even if that leads into dangerous waters?"

He eyed her shrewdly. "Anything that requires a leap of faith involves a certain amount of danger, Jess. That's true of forgiveness. And trust. And love."

Jess turned and gazed out again over the placid lake, wishing some of its serenity would seep into her soul. She tucked her hair behind her ear and drew a steadying breath. "Can I tell you something in confidence?"

"Of course."

"Sometimes I—I think I'm falling in love again with Scott," she whispered.

"Is that bad?" he asked gently.

She looked at him in confusion. "I don't know. It feels wrong somehow, like I'm dishonoring the memory of Elizabeth by accepting back into my life the man who caused her death."

Reverend Young studied her for a moment. "You know, Jess, I visited Scott regularly when he was in prison. We had a lot of long talks. Many of them about Elizabeth. And I lost track of the number of times he broke down and wept bitterly over her death. I can tell you with absolute certainty that no man ever loved his daughter more than Scott. Her loss was as devastating to him as it was to you. So I don't really think there's a conflict between your feelings for Scott and your love for Elizabeth. In fact, I believe that one of the best ways for you to honor the memory of Elizabeth would be to love her father—who loved her with all his heart."

Jess stared at Reverend Young. Could he possibly be right? she wondered in shock. Was loving Scott respectful of—rather than a violation of—the memory of Elizabeth? Or was the minister telling her this just because he was looking out for Scott's best interests? Yet she saw only conviction and honesty in the man's eyes. Dear God, she wanted to believe him! Desperately! Because if she did, there would be one less worry on her mind. One less obstacle to forgiveness. And she would be one step closer to making peace with her past.

"You don't have to make any decisions until you're ready," Reverend Young reassured her with an understanding smile. "Just think about it. Pray about it. And answers will come—in God's time." He stood and reached out to take her hand in a warm clasp. "I'll keep you in my prayers. And now I'll leave you to enjoy this beautiful spot in peace."

Jess watched the minister disappear down the flagstone path, then turned back to the quiet lake. Peace. Even the word had a lovely sound, she thought wistfully, savoring the echo of it in her mind. For four years it had been absent from her vocabulary. And from her life. In fact, she'd begun to believe that it had disappeared forever.

But suddenly, for the first time in a very long while, she felt the stirrings of hope in her heart. Reverend Young's comments had given her new insights and new options about how to deal with her situation. And if he was right, maybe she would find—through reconciliation—the peace that had been so elusive.

Now she just needed the courage to follow her heart.

"...heard the latest about Scott Mitchell?"

"I knew he got out."

"That's not the half of it. Get this...he and Jess are living together!"

Jess stopped abruptly, hidden by a bank of greenery from the women whose conversation she had inadvertently overheard at the restaurant where she was meeting Scott for lunch. She recognized the voices—the wives of two of Scott's former business associates with whom she and Scott had gone out socially on a number of occasions.

"You're kidding! Why in the world would she take up with him again? He's an ex-con, for heaven's sake!"

"I have no idea. She could certainly do better than that. I mean, what can he offer her? His career is toast. Brian saw him planting flowers at an office building downtown. He must work for a nursery or something. Manual labor—do you believe it? Which probably pays dirt—pardon the pun."

The other woman chuckled. "Cute. Anyway, that's probably all he could get. After all, who'd want to hire an ex-con?"

"Yeah. So much for the good life. No more power lunches or country clubs or filet mignon for him."

"Not exactly the fast track."

"Not exactly *any* track."

"Oh, I don't know. Maybe one day he could move up to shrubs. Or even shade trees. Or maybe Jess could support him."

Jess had become increasingly incensed as she listened to the conversation, but the two women's laughter was what drove her over the edge. Without even stopping to think, she stepped around the greenery.

"Hello, Jennifer. Susan." It was a struggle, but somehow she managed to maintain a civil tone.

"Jess! Why…we were just talking about you," one of the women replied, clearly flustered. She exchanged a guilty look with her companion, and both women's faces grew pink.

At least they had the grace to look embarrassed, Jess

thought, gritting her teeth. "I know. I couldn't help overhearing. And I wanted to set the record straight on a few things. First of all, Scott and I are not living together—at least, not in the way you think. Second, Scott understands that material things aren't really what life's about—and that they have nothing to do with what a person has to 'offer.' So the amount of money he makes isn't that important to him. It's too bad more people don't have their priorities straight," she said, glancing pointedly at the diamond rings on the women's fingers and the BMW key chain lying on the table.

"As for manual labor," she continued, "it's a lot more honest than the backbiting politics of the corporate world. And finally, I would suggest you think about your attitude toward ex-cons. You know one now. So you ought to realize that they don't all fit the same mold. Writing people off, denying them a chance because of a stereotype—be it race or gender or age or a prison record—is just plain wrong." She paused and took a deep breath. "Enjoy your lunch, ladies."

Jess didn't wait for them to reply. She simply turned and walked toward her table, her head held high. Only when she sat, her back to the women, did she realize that her legs felt like rubber and her hands were trembling. In-your-face confrontation just wasn't her style, she acknowledged, drawing a shaky breath. She generally avoided it at all costs, unless she felt passionate about a subject.

Which ought to tell her something, she suddenly realized with a jolt. Because her last two confrontations had involved defending Scott.

* * *

Scott's throat tightened with emotion and he moved farther back into the shadows as he watched Jess walk to her table. He, too, had overheard the conversation between the two women they'd once considered friends. Frankly, he was getting used to dealing with that kind of garbage. It rarely bothered him anymore. What did bother him was that their derogatory comments hadn't been confined to him. By association, Jess had been tainted, as well. Which was something he simply hadn't considered when he'd thought about them reuniting.

Scott jammed his hands into his pockets as he studied Jess's profile. She was clearly upset. He could see it in the rapid rise and fall of her chest, in the way she tucked her hair behind her ear, in her white-knuckled grip on her water glass. But intuitively he knew she wasn't upset because of the women's disparaging comments about *her*. She was upset because of what they'd said about *him*. Which made him feel good. And bad.

On the plus side, her vigorous defense of him was clear evidence that her feelings for him were deepening—whether she realized it or not.

On the minus side, today was only a preview of what she'd have to deal with if they got back together. Scott recalled her father's comment a few days earlier. "If you cared for her at all, you'd leave her alone. You'd walk out of her life and never come back," he'd said. Scott hadn't believed him then. But suddenly a seed of doubt crept into his mind. Was it fair to subject Jess to the bias that would likely follow him the rest of his life? he wondered, a troubled frown furrowing his brow. He'd just seen the effect of it first-hand. Her righteous anger told him that she was able to deal with such prejudice publicly. But as he studied her now, he was also aware that it had bruised her heart. This time, on his behalf. But eventually she would feel the hurt for herself, as well.

"Excuse me, sir...can I help you?"

Scott turned to find a waiter at his elbow. "No, thanks. I'm just getting ready to join my party."

As the man disappeared, Scott took a deep breath. Hiding in the shadows wasn't going to give him any answers. If he'd learned anything at all over the past four years it was to acknowledge problems and deal with them head-on. So, forcing his lips into a smile, he stepped into the sunlight and made his way toward Jess.

She looked up as he approached and returned his smile, though he could still see evidence of strain on her face as he took the seat across from her.

"Sorry I'm a few minutes late," he apologized. "A long-winded customer."

"That's okay. It gave me time to make a quick trip to the ladies' room."

"That's what I figured. The hostess said you'd been seated on the patio, but you were nowhere to be seen when I got here. So I waited under the grape arbor."

She shifted uncomfortably and glanced over her shoulder toward the table where the two women had been seated.

"They made a fast exit after your conversation."

Her gaze swung back to his. "How much did you hear?"

"Enough. And I'd like to thank you for your spirited defense."

Her face colored slightly. "I can't believe the things they were saying! How can people be so…so…"

"Unkind?"

Her eyebrows rose. "I had a stronger word in mind."

A wry smile pulled at the corners of his lips. "I'm getting used to it, Jess. It goes with the territory of being an ex-con."

"Well, it shouldn't."

"I agree. But it does. And unfortunately, the stigma is transferred to people who associate with ex-cons. Frankly, I don't care what those women said about me. But I do care very much about their derogatory comments about you."

She looked at him blankly. "What do you mean?" she asked, confirming his suspicion that she hadn't even noticed their snide remarks about her. He hated to call attention to them, but she needed to be aware of what she would face if the two of them got back together.

"Their implications were pretty clear," he said soberly. "You must be crazy to take up with an ex-con. It was beneath you. There's nothing I could offer you. You might even end up supporting me."

She stared at him. "I heard some of that. Not all."

"Trust me, it was there. Ex-cons become very sensitive to those kinds of things."

She looked at him, appalled. "Do you run into this all the time?"

He shrugged. "I was warned about it, so I was prepared. For myself, anyway. But not for you," he replied, evading her question.

She dismissed his concern with an impatient shake of her head. "I can handle that kind of garbage," she said brusquely.

"I know. I saw you in action. But I'd rather you didn't have to. And unfortunately, if you hang around me you'll have to," he said evenly, his gaze locked with hers.

Though his manner was outwardly relaxed, Jess could feel his tension. Clearly, he was deeply concerned about the scene that had just transpired—and even more concerned that it would likely be repeated in the future. Far more concerned than she. And he needed to know that. She returned his gaze steadily, and when she spoke her voice was filled with quiet resolve. "I'm not going to live my life to accommodate other people's prejudices. If people are so shallow they can't look past stereotypes, that's their problem, not mine. And if they can't accept me for who I am— the choices I make, the people I..." She had almost said "love," she realized in shock, her breath lodging in her throat. She stared at Scott, who was watching her intently, and quickly changed direction. "The people I choose to include in my life—then I don't want to have anything to do with them. And as for people like Jennifer and Susan—frankly, they're not even worth wasting breath on."

Scott studied her, warmed and encouraged by her

response. Clearly, her feelings on the subject were strong. But were they strong enough to stand repeated attacks? he wondered. Including those from her own parents? Would she eventually become disheartened— or would her convictions intensify in adversity? Unfortunately, Scott didn't know the answer. He'd just have to trust his heart on this one, he realized—and pray that the Lord would offer him guidance.

"Can I take your order?"

Jess and Scott simultaneously looked at the waiter, then at each other.

"I'm ready, but you've hardly had a chance to look at the menu," Jess said.

He glanced down and scanned it quickly. "Go ahead. I only need a second."

Jess turned back to the waiter. "I'll have a chicken Caesar salad."

Scott looked at her with a frown. To get her to accept his invitation for this "thanks-for-your-hospitality" lunch, he'd had to overcome her protests that it was both unnecessary and too expensive. Though she'd finally capitulated, the cost was clearly still on her mind. "Don't you want something more substantial than that?" he said.

"This is plenty, really. I usually just have yogurt for lunch, so this is a big meal for me," she replied truthfully.

For a moment Scott hesitated, but then he let it pass and gave his own order. "Actually, as it turns out, this lunch is not only a thank-you but a celebration," he said as he handed his menu to the waiter.

She looked at him in surprise. "How so?"

"I have some good news. I found an apartment."

Jess stared at him. If his news was so good, why had her stomach suddenly dropped to her toes? she wondered. "Th-that's great," she replied, striving for an enthusiastic tone.

"I stopped in to see it this morning on my way to work. I think even Karen would approve. There is one problem, though. It won't be ready for occupancy for a week."

Though she quickly masked it, Scott saw the relief in her eyes—and suddenly felt the same emotion sweep through his heart. She didn't want him to leave!

"You're welcome to stay on at my place," she replied, confirming his assessment.

He smiled at her, and the warmth that radiated from his eyes sent a flush of heat sweeping over her. "I was hoping you'd say that. Because there's nowhere else I'd rather be. Thank you." He reached over and covered her hand with his.

Her breath caught in her throat as she looked at his lean brown fingers resting on hers. It took a concerted effort to tear her gaze from their hands, but when she finally did the undisguised hunger in his eyes not only made her mouth go dry—it curled her toes.

And made her wonder if she'd just made a big mistake.

"Wow! Something smells great!" Scott called as he stepped through the front door. "I hope I got what you wanted. I had no idea ginger came in—"

"Happy birthday!"

Scott paused, speechless, on the threshold of the

kitchen. Today had *started* with a surprise, when Jess had said she'd like to go to church with him. And now it was *ending* with one, as well. The significance of the day had fleetingly crossed his mind when he'd awakened this morning, but then he'd forgotten about it. Frankly, his birthday had passed pretty much without notice for the past four years, except for a card from Karen and her family. He'd certainly never expected Jess to mark the occasion. And yet she had obviously gone out of her way to make the day special, to the point of contriving an errand so she could prepare a surprise while he was gone.

His gaze moved from the table set with crisp linens and good china to the chocolate cake on the counter dotted with far too many candles, then on to the gaily wrapped package beside it. Finally it returned to Jess, who was watching him anxiously, her face slightly flushed.

A rush of tenderness washed over him, and he reached up to brush the back of his hand across his suddenly damp eyes. "I can't believe…I never expected… This is so…" He paused and cleared his throat. "So much for eloquence," he said with a shaky laugh. "What I'm trying to say is thank you."

Jess smiled nervously. "You're welcome. I made pork tenderloin. I know you used to like it. I hope it's okay. I haven't made it in…for a long time."

If he was a man given to impulse, Jess would be in his arms by now, Scott thought. But he was still treading on somewhat shaky ground, and a wrong move could blow all the progress he'd made so far, he reminded himself, silently repeating the mantra he'd adopted over the past few days as logic and need duked it out in his heart. *Don't rush her. Wait until she reaches out to you. Be grateful for whatever she offers.* It was sound advice. But it was getting harder and harder to follow.

"Pork tenderloin sounds wonderful," he said huskily.

She tucked her hair behind her ear. "Well, have a seat. It's ready."

He did as instructed, and though the meal started off a bit awkwardly, his light banter quickly put her at ease. By the time they got to the cake, she was completely relaxed.

"I think you put too many candles on this," he protested with a smile as she placed it in front of him. "It's going to set off your fire alarm."

She chuckled. "I don't think so. Now make a wish."

It was what she'd always said on birthdays. But the last word faded out as their gazes locked. Because Scott had only one wish. And they both knew what it was. Without breaking eye contact he slowly leaned down and blew until every candle was out.

Again he was tempted to reach for her. Again he refrained. But it took every ounce of his self-restraint.

There was silence for a moment, and when she spoke her voice was a bit too bright—and breathless. "Well...that was impressive. I could say something about lots of hot air, but I won't." She lifted the cake to the counter behind her, turning her back as she cut it. "Why don't we take our cake and coffee into the living room?"

"Okay." He stood as well and reached for their plates. "I'll just clean up a little first so we don't have this mess to come back to."

She turned, the cake knife in her hand. Since becoming her house guest he'd made it a point to take on clean-up chores after meals, but tonight she shook her head. "Not on your birthday," she said firmly.

He hesitated, then grinned and put the plates back on the table. "Since you have a knife in your hand, I don't think I'll argue. Can I at least carry the cake into the living room?"

She nodded, handing him the two plates. "I'll get the coffee."

When she joined him a moment later carrying two mugs, she also had the wrapped package under her arm. She handed him his coffee, then sat beside him on the couch and held out the present.

"You didn't have to do this, Jess," he said, hesitating.

She shrugged. "I wanted to. Go ahead. Open it."

He reached for the package then, and she scooted closer to look over his shoulder as he tore off the wrapping to reveal a comprehensive landscaping book.

"I asked some of the horticulturists at the garden to recommend a good reference book," she said anxiously. "This was their unanimous choice. I—I hope it's all right. I can return it if you don't think it will be helpful."

Scott ran his hand lovingly over the dust jacket, trying to swallow past the lump in his throat as he vainly attempted to think of something he could say that would adequately express what was in his heart.

But finally he gave up. Mere words couldn't capture the depth of his feelings for this special woman, for her thoughtfulness and her kindness and her incredibly loving heart.

He turned to her, and her eyes were so close he could see the gold flecks in their irises. So close that he began to drown in their green depths. So close that logic somehow seemed less important than listening to his heart. And his heart was speaking loud and clear, telling him to forget about words and express his feelings in the silent language of love.

It was time, his heart said with quiet certainty.

And Scott listened to his heart.

Chapter Twelve

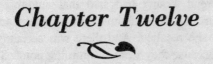

Slowly, ever so slowly, Scott set the book aside and reached out to gently touch Jess's cheek. He heard her breath catch as his fingers made contact, and then she went absolutely still, like a tensed deer unsure whether to linger or bolt. Warning bells went off in Scott's mind, but he was powerless to heed them. Now that he'd touched Jess, there was simply no way he could back off.

Lightly, brushing her skin with only the tips of his fingers, he began to stroke her cheek. Her eyes fluttered closed, and though a tremor ran through her she didn't pull away. Even when he let his fingers travel to the curve of her neck, when he gently pushed aside her soft hair to trace the delicate curve of her ear, she remained unmoving. Only when his fingers returned to her face and whispered across her soft lips did she jerk back with a gasp, her eyes wide.

Jess stared at Scott. She'd known all along that the chemistry between them was as potent as ever. She'd tried to ignore it, tried to dance around it, tried to pretend she could control her reaction to it. But that was no longer possible. Scott's undemanding, gentle touch had ignited a feeling that simply could not be ignored. Every nerve in her body was tingling, and her pulse rate was off the scale. She wanted this. Needed this. But she was scared.

Reverend Young had said that anything that required a leap of faith involved a certain amount of danger, she recalled. And there was certainly danger here—because they were at a turning point. She could walk away, insulate herself in the relatively safe but lonely world she'd created, or she could take that leap of faith, trusting that her heart—and the Lord—would guide her steps.

As she looked into Scott's deep brown eyes, she knew what she *wanted* to do. She wanted to melt into his embrace, let his strong, sheltering arms carry her to a world where only the two of them existed. Where they could soar together to a place of joy and peace and harmony. Where nothing mattered but the love that bound them together. That's what she wanted—if she could just get past the doubt and fear.

With an effort she pulled her gaze from his and transferred it to the picture of Elizabeth. Fear hadn't been part of her daughter's vocabulary, she recalled with a wistful pang. Elizabeth had always wanted to climb to the highest spot on the jungle gym while her mother watched in trepidation from below, ready to cushion her fall if she lost her balance or took a wrong step. Jess had repeatedly cautioned her to be careful, a warning that usually fell on deaf ears. But suddenly as clearly as if it had been spoken yesterday, the response her daughter had once made to that admonition came back to her.

"I *am* being careful, Mommy. But if you're too careful you can never touch the sky," Elizabeth had said matter-of-factly, in all of her four-year-old wisdom.

Tonight Jess wanted to touch the sky. Or at least take the first step up the jungle gym. But there was no one waiting to catch her if she fell, as there had been for her daughter. Yet she knew beyond the shadow of a doubt that the lack of a safety net wouldn't have stopped Elizabeth. So the question was, did she share her daughter's courage?

Scott watched Jess as she gazed at the picture of their daughter, fully aware that she was struggling with a decision that would have dramatic implications for both of them. He remained motionless, barely daring to breathe, his hand resting in his lap where he'd let it drop when she'd abruptly backed off. For four long years he'd dreamed of the moment when he would again hold the woman he loved in his arms, the moment she would come to him willingly and say, if not "I love you," at least, "I'll give this a chance." And now the moment seemed near. So near that he began to tremble. And to pray.

Jess took a deep breath, trying vainly to control the uncomfortable pounding of her heart as she looked back at Scott. His gaze captured hers compellingly, revealing a myriad of emotions. Tenderness. Love. Encouragement. Hope. Passion. Most definitely passion, she acknowledged as her mouth went dry. The banked fire in his eyes was carefully held in check, but she knew that it would burst into a consuming flame at the slightest provocation. Yet he didn't say a word or make a move. He simply waited, leaving the outcome in her hands.

Jess thought again of Elizabeth, always reaching for the sky. Never letting fear get in the way. And with sudden decision, she slowly, tentatively reached out and touched his face.

His eyes darkened, and now it was his turn to suck in a sharp breath. But he remained otherwise motionless—which gave Jess the courage to continue.

Lightly, gently she let her fingers move over his face, revisiting the familiar contours, learning the changes. His brow was no longer as smooth as it had once been, she realized. But worry and pain and sorrow could do that to a person. A muscle in his cheek clenched as her hand drifted lower to graze the taut skin over his cheekbones. Then her fingers moved lower still to trace the line of his strong jaw. It was just as she remembered it, complete with the slightly rough texture that signaled the beginning of evening stubble—a tactile sensation that had always given her pleasure. Only when her fingers approached his lips did she hesitate.

Jess's touch had been pleasurable torture, and it had taken every ounce of Scott's willpower to remain unmoving as she explored his face. But now that she'd hesitated, he reacted. Slowly, deliberately he reached for her hand and guided it to his lips, placing an exquisitely tender kiss in her palm. When he raised his gaze to hers, he made no attempt to hide the love in his eyes. Nor could she hide the longing in the depths of hers, though doubt still hovered at the edges. But he wasn't going to give doubt a chance to get the upper hand. Not tonight. Not when he was a whisper away from making a reality of the dream that had sustained him in prison.

So before she had a chance for second thoughts he reached out to her, cupping her face with both hands, letting his callused thumbs gently stroke her satiny skin. He could feel her quivering, and he knew that she was afraid. But he also knew that fear alone wasn't the cause of her reaction. And that gave him hope.

As he drank in the sight of her beautiful face and felt her soft skin beneath his fingers, a wave of gratitude and tenderness and love washed over him, so intense that tears pricked his eyelids and his throat tightened with emotion. "I love you, Jess," he whispered hoarsely. "I always have and I always will."

He watched her eyes grow luminous, then fill with answering tears. And when he pulled her close, pressing her soft, supple body tightly against the hard, muscular planes of his own, she offered no resistance. He buried his face in her soft hair, and for a long time he simply held her, savoring the moment that for four long years had been only a fantasy. He could feel her trembling—or was it him? he wondered. He felt as shaky as a teenager about to experience his first kiss. Except the stakes were a whole lot higher in this case.

At last he eased back far enough to search Jess's slightly dazed eyes. Doubt had been replaced by yearning. And invitation. And need. And so he did what he'd been wanting to do ever since he'd seen her that first day outside her condo. He lowered his mouth to hers to taste the sweetness that only her kiss could offer.

As Scott's lips moved over hers, gently at first and then with growing urgency, Jess's world spun out of orbit. For four long years she'd stifled memories of the radiant joy of being in Scott's embrace. Of the way his strong arms would mold her pliant body to his, firmly, surely, possessively, but with infinite tenderness even at the moments of greatest passion. Even now, after four lonely years, when he must be yearning for so much more than this simple kiss, his touch was demanding but not forceful. She could taste his hunger, feel his need, and she knew what he wanted. But she also knew that he would be grateful for whatever she was willing to give. And that made her feel safe. Which, in turn, only made her want to give more.

Scott knew the precise instant at which Jess let down her guard and gave herself to the moment. He could feel her surrender in the subtle change in muscle tension, in the way her body melted against his. And as she proceeded to meet him kiss for kiss, as her hands moved convulsively over his back, up to his neck, urging him closer and closer, only one rational thought penetrated his consciousness—the dreams that had sustained him in his cold, sterile cell didn't even come close to actually holding Jess's warm, responsive body in his arms.

When Scott at last drew back, they were both breathing fast. Too fast. For several long seconds that was the only sound in the room as they both struggled to regain their equilibrium. But slowly they came back to earth. And as they did, Scott saw the doubt and uncertainty creep back into Jess's eyes. And heard it in her voice.

"Scott, I…I didn't plan for…I mean, I don't want you to think that… I'm still not sure…" Her voice trailed off, and warm color suffused her face.

He studied her for a moment, then reached over and took her hand. "Let me put your mind at ease," he said, his voice slightly unsteady. "I don't consider tonight a promise or a commitment. Just a first step. Okay?"

Relief flooded her eyes, and she nodded jerkily. "Okay." She drew a deep breath, then looked at the table. "I—I'm afraid our coffee got cold. And we didn't eat our cake."

He looked at her steadily. "No. But I got my wish."

As for the coffee, it was the only thing in the room that *had* grown cold, he thought wryly as his remark sent another becoming blush across Jess's cheeks. And suddenly he was glad he'd found an apartment. Because he knew he still needed to move slowly. And after tonight, that was going to be very, very difficult. Especially when he wanted to share so much more than a roof with the woman he loved.

"Got a minute, Scott?"

Scott looked up from his clipboard to find Seth standing at the entrance of the tropical house. "Sure. I'm about done with the inventory in here anyway."

"Let's sit for a minute, then." Seth nodded to a teakwood bench tucked under a display of palms.

Scott watched in surprise as the older man headed

toward the bench. The only time Seth ever sat was in his office, and even that was a rarity. The man seemed to have an inexhaustible supply of energy, and he was constantly on the move. Unless he had something serious to discuss.

Scott frowned. Had his boss noticed his preoccupation this week? he wondered as he followed him to the bench. Because ever since his birthday, he'd been distracted. Big time. There'd been no more kissing, but the tension between him and Jess fairly sizzled. It took every ounce of his willpower to keep his hands to himself, and on the few occasions when he simply hadn't been able to resist the urge to reach out and touch her, sparks had flown in all directions. Keeping himself in check had become a major battle.

Adding to that had been other, more practical concerns that he'd pushed aside until now. Like the need to contribute financially to a relationship. Like making enough money to support a family, if the Lord were to bless him with other children. Seth had been good to him and he loved the work, but even if he kept moving up at the nursery, it would be a long time before his wages would be sufficient to provide for a family. And the idea of reentering the corporate world—even if that was possible—held no appeal.

As Scott sat on the bench, Seth leaned back, chewing speculatively on his cigar. "In case I haven't said it already, I want to thank you for the marketing advice. Those ads you put together with that agency are paying big dividends. Gross revenue is up twenty percent since they started running. Which means we're twenty percent busier. Too busy for me to handle alone. I could use a partner. You interested?''

Scott stared at the older man, dumbfounded. He had grown accustomed to the owner's abrupt style and rapid-fire delivery, but today's bombshell left him reeling.

Seth's eyes glinted with amusement and the corners of his lips quirked up. "I guess maybe that was a little too blunt. But I'm not a man who likes to waste words. Get to the point and get on with it is my motto. Good thing I didn't go into politics, I guess." He leaned back on the bench and crossed his arms over his chest.

Usually Scott appreciated the man's wry wit and dry sense of humor. But he was so busy trying to assimilate Seth's first comment that he barely heard the second one. "You want me to be your partner?" Scott said incredulously when he finally found his voice.

"That's right."

"But…why me?"

Seth chomped on his cigar and eyed him shrewdly. "You're smart. You're a hard worker. You're honest. You have a knack for this business. Seems like a winning combination to me. So are you interested?"

Scott raked his fingers through his hair as a wave of excitement washed over him. Maybe he had a future here after all. Seth's offer would allow him to do the work he loved for the rest of his life *and* provide him with a decent standard of living. But Scott's euphoria quickly faded as a strong dose of reality suddenly kicked in. Partnerships cost money. Which he didn't have, he acknowledged with a sigh. "I'm definitely interested. But unfortunately I can't afford to buy into the business,'' he said regretfully.

Seth shrugged. ''We can work things out. I could put together an equity deal that would let you work toward half ownership over time.''

Once again Scott stared at him, completely taken aback by the man's kindness and generosity. ''You're serious, aren't you?''

''Wouldn't have said it if I wasn't,'' Seth replied gruffly, though the affection in his eyes belied his tone. ''But don't make any snap decisions. This is a hard business. Takes a lot of energy and stamina to keep things on an even keel. It's a good business, though. Working with living things, creating places of beauty—that's healthy for the soul. Keeps you in touch with God's creation. So think about it overnight. And if you're still interested in the morning, we'll talk about the particulars.''

Seth stood, and Scott followed. The older man was slightly shorter than Scott, and much more wiry in build. But there was strength in his muscles, and character in his face. Their eyes met, Seth's startlingly blue, Scott's deep brown. And though they came from entirely different backgrounds, each man recognized in the other a kindred spirit. Each knew that their shared values and mutual respect would provide a solid foundation on which to build. And Scott also knew that he could never form a partnership with a finer man. He held out his hand, and Seth took it in a firm grip.

''Thank you.'' The words were simple but heartfelt.

"It's my pleasure, Scott. Good people deserve good things. I'm just doing my part."

Scott flipped on the evening news, then headed for the kitchen. Jess had called to say she'd be a little late, and she'd sounded so tired that in a moment of madness he'd offered to start dinner. Though he'd gotten very good at most household chores, cooking was definitely not one of them, he acknowledged ruefully. Still, he could at least get the salad going. After all, how much damage could he do to lettuce?

As he absently withdrew the ingredients from the refrigerator he thought back to Jess's reaction when he'd told her about Seth's offer, and a smile tipped the corners of his lips. She'd clearly been delighted for him—and proud. It had been a good moment. One that had led to a spontaneous kiss—of joy and congratulations and celebration rather than passion, but a good kiss nonetheless. One that was comfortable and natural and warm. The kind that couples often shared after years of marriage. The kind *they* had once shared—and which had sometimes led to other ways of celebrating. This one hadn't. But it was another step forward. And it gave Scott hope that Jess was on the verge of stepping out of the past and into the future—with him. Though he would be moving in two days, he was optimistic that before long their separation would be history. That they could once again...

"...identified as Juan Ruelas, who was released from prison in April after serving ten years of a fifteen-year sentence for involuntary manslaughter. More on this story when we return."

With a frown, Scott left the salad fixings on the counter and moved into the living room. He knew Juan Ruelas. They'd served together. The man had been a loner, rarely talking to other inmates, but for some reason he'd taken a liking to Scott. Maybe because they both came from St. Louis. But more likely because Scott was willing to listen when the man wanted to vent about his growing-up years in the slums, about his absentee father and alcoholic mother, about stealing food when he was nine years old because there was nothing to eat in the house, about his bitterness toward a society that seemed to offer little hope and even fewer opportunities. He would pour out his feelings in a rush of words, like water suddenly released from behind a dam. Scott could do little to ease his pain—except listen. But that had often seemed to be enough.

Scott had known Juan might be released in the spring and that he, too, planned to return to St. Louis. He'd meant to follow up, to let the troubled man know that he still had a friend if things got tough. But his own transition back into society had been fraught with more challenges than he'd anticipated and he'd never gotten around to looking Juan up. Now it appeared to be too late. Though he'd missed the first part of the teaser for the news, if Juan was the lead story he was in big trouble.

The commercial break ended, and the anchorman came back on the screen. "Earlier this afternoon Judge Walter Johnson was taken hostage at his office in the county courthouse by a man he sentenced to prison ten years ago. According to witnesses, Juan Ruelas gained access to the courthouse about four o'clock this afternoon through a service entrance and made his way to Judge Johnson's office. He released the judge's secretary, who told police that Johnson had two handguns and that he appeared extremely agitated. He is demanding one hundred thousand dollars in cash, an airline ticket to Mexico and safe passage to the airport in return for the release of Judge Johnson. The police have been negotiating with him by phone, but so far there has been no progress. We'll keep you informed as developments occur.

"In other news tonight…"

With a troubled frown Scott reached over and slowly turned off the television. The police would get nowhere with Juan. He hated authority figures of any kind, particularly those in law enforcement, whose mere presence seemed to incite his already volatile emotions. Only someone he trusted would have a chance of reaching him, of convincing him to give up this crazy scheme. Only someone like Scott.

"Is something wrong?"

He turned, startled, to find Jess hovering in the doorway. He hadn't heard her come in, but he could tell from her expression that she'd been standing there long enough to sense that something was *very* wrong. Her hand was white-knuckled on the door frame, and every line of her body was tense.

Scott drew a shaky breath. *Dear God, why?* he cried in silent anguish as the full impact of the news story suddenly hit home. *Just when I'm about to regain my life, I'm faced with a situation where I might lose it. And yet I can't just walk away. Not when another life hangs in the balance. A life I might be able to save. If Juan is as agitated as it sounds, there's no one else who even stands a chance of calming him down enough to talk him out of this plan. It's up to me. And I could very well fail. Please, Lord, give me the courage to do what I have to do. And please help Jess understand why I must.*

Slowly Scott walked toward Jess—and the closer he came, the more scared she got. There was pain in his eyes. And fear. And resignation. But there was also love. Deep, abiding love that reached all the way to the depths of her soul. She clung to that love as Scott reached out and took her cold hands in his.

"Did you see the story about the judge?" he asked quietly.

She nodded mutely, not trusting her voice.

"I served with the man who took him hostage. In a sense, I became his confidant. He's a troubled soul, Jess, with a lot of anger inside. I don't know what made him do this, but I do know that he must be desperate. And he's not going to listen to the police. He'll only listen to someone he trusts."

The knot in her stomach tightened convulsively, and her voice was strained when she spoke. "His social worker, maybe?"

Scott shook his head regretfully. "Unfortunately, no. He or she is part of the 'system' Juan hates. It has to be a friend."

Jess drew a shuddering breath. She knew where this was leading. Had known almost since she'd stepped into the room. "You can talk to him by phone, can't you?'' There was a touch of desperation in her voice now.

Scott saw the fear in her eyes, and it matched that in his heart. He wished he could just walk away from this, pretend he'd never heard the news story. But it wasn't in his nature. "We can try that first," he said carefully, knowing that wasn't what she wanted to hear, but reluctant to make any promises he might not be able to keep. Because he doubted that a long-distance conversation would have much impact with Juan. But he would try. For Jess's sake. And his own.

Jess took refuge in the protective circle of Scott's arms as he made his call to the police, drawing comfort from the solid strength of his lean body. She watched him as he spoke, his voice calm, his resolution firm. And although she was deathly afraid, she was also proud. Of his caring. His convictions. His compassion.

And suddenly, as if a veil had been lifted, she realized that all her doubts about this special man were groundless. Over and over again during the past few months he'd demonstrated how his life had been transformed by the power of God's grace, had proven that he was a man worthy not only of forgiveness—but of love. Jess had simply been too blind—or perhaps too hard-hearted—to recognize that the changes in Scott were real, just as his remorse was. And now that she had, it might be too late.

Scott replaced the receiver and turned to her, taking both her hands tenderly in his. "They're sending a squad car. I'll be back as soon as it's over," he said gently.

She shook her head. "I can't just sit here and wait for the phone to ring. I'm going with you."

He frowned. "I'll feel better if you're here."

"But I won't. I'm going."

The stubborn set of her chin told him that argument was useless. And he didn't want to spend these last few moments arguing, anyway. Silently he reached for her, and she went willingly into his arms, hugging him fiercely.

"Oh, Scott, why did this have to happen now?" she asked brokenly, her voice muffled against his shirt.

"I don't know," he admitted, his lips in her hair, his own voice none too steady.

They clung to one another silently, all too aware that in a few minutes Scott would walk into a situation fraught with danger and uncertainty. And equally aware that he might not walk out. For Jess, it was like a replay of the nightmare events of four years before. Now, as then, her life was in chaos, pummeled by forces she didn't control. But this time, instead of closing herself off from the Lord she reached out to Him, praying for the strength and courage to accept His will.

When the doorbell rang, a sob rose in Jess's throat and she instinctively hugged Scott even more tightly. Only at the second, more insistent ring did he ease back and look down at her. Tears were running freely down her face, and the anguish and fear in her eyes tore at his heart. "I have to go," he said gently.

"I know," she whispered brokenly. She reached up to lay her hand against his cheek for a moment, then cupped his neck and drew his head down to hers. And in the instant before their lips met in a last, desperate kiss, he heard her whisper four beautiful words.

"I love you, Scott."

"We told him you were on the way. He's on the line. Good luck."

As Scott took the phone from the officer he glanced toward the cordoned-off courthouse, where a man's life hung in the balance. *Please, Lord give me the words—and the courage—to see this through,* he prayed fervently.

"Juan?"

"Hey, Scott, is that really you, man?"

Juan's voice was so agitated that Scott hardly recognized it. He had seen the man rant and rave on numerous occasions, but from his high-pitched, frenzied tone it was clear that Juan was over the top today, high on either drugs or fear. Though his heart was hammering in his chest, Scott kept his voice as calm as possible when he responded. "Yeah. It's me. What's going on?"

"I got me a judge."

"So I hear. What do you want a judge for?"

"I don't want him, man. He's just a ticket out of here. I'm heading for Mexico."

"I thought you were going to go straight when you got out."

"Yeah, well, it didn't work out that way," he said bitterly. "Nobody wants an ex-con around. They treat you like dirt. Like you still got the smell of prison on you. Ain't no such thing as a second chance, man."

"There might be, if you let the judge go. I can talk to the police for you."

A brief, harsh laugh came over the line. "Who you tryin' to kid, man? They'll throw me back in that hole and I won't never see the light of day again. I can't go back there. This is my only—" A click sounded on the line, and Juan stopped talking for a moment. "Hey, man, what was that noise? Is somebody listening in?" he asked suspiciously.

"No. It's just me and you."

"Yeah, well, I'm not talkin' on the phone anymore. You wanna talk, you come up here. Alone."

The line went dead.

Slowly Scott handed the phone back to one of several police officers who were now clustered around him. "He wants me to come up."

"No!" The panic in Jess's voice—and eyes—was almost palpable as she reached out to clutch his arm.

"I agree with the lady, Mr. Mitchell," one of the officers said. "That guy's on the edge. And he could slip over at any moment."

"He won't hurt me," Scott said with more confidence than he felt.

One of the higher-ranking officers stepped forward. "I don't think it's worth the risk. We could end up with two dead men instead of one," he said bluntly.

Scott heard Jess gasp, and he reached for her hand and held it tightly. But he didn't look at her. If he did, his courage would fail. "He won't hurt me," Scott repeated. "I know Juan. He trusts me. And there's a chance he'll listen to me. If he doesn't, you're no worse off than you are now. You really don't have anything to lose.''

The officer looked at him skeptically. ''You mean you think he'll just let you walk out of there after your little chat?''

Scott's gaze locked with his. ''I'm betting my life on it,'' he replied steadily.

The man studied him for a moment, then brushed a weary hand across his eyes. ''I don't know what else to try, other than rushing the building. And we're bound to have some casualties if we do that.'' He sighed and turned to one of the officers. ''Okay. Get Ruelas on the phone again. Tell him his friend is coming up.'' Then he turned back to Scott and pointed toward the building. ''It's the corner office. Second floor. The one with the broken glass. He took a potshot at us earlier. I guess he wanted to let us know he was serious.''

As Scott glanced toward the window that had been shattered by a bullet, his courage faltered. Dear God, he didn't want to do this! But the cup had been given to him. He had no choice but to accept it. Slowly he turned to Jess, and his gut clenched painfully as his gaze took in her pale face, trembling hands and shock-filled eyes. He reached for her and pulled her close, cradling her head with his hand as he pressed her cheek to his chest, wanting to spare her this but knowing he couldn't.

''I'll be back,'' he whispered, his voice muffled in her hair.

And then, before she could respond, he gently extricated himself from her arms and strode toward the building, leaving his fate in the hands of the Lord.

From the moment Scott disappeared inside the courthouse, time crawled for Jess. Five minutes felt like an hour. Ten minutes felt like a year. Twenty minutes felt like an eternity. After half an hour, she was so distraught that one of the officers brought her a bottle of water and urged her to sit down. But she refused both. Her throat was too tight to swallow, and she was too hyper to remain still. So she paced. And prayed. And kept her gaze fixed on the second-floor window.

After forty-five minutes, even the police were getting uneasy. There'd been no communication from the building, and a phone call to the judge's office had gone unanswered. Jess's nerves were ready to snap, and she was just about to demand that the police do something—*anything*—when at last the silence was broken.

By a single gunshot.

Jess's heart stopped, then lurched on, and she felt physically sick. Pandemonium broke out around her as the officer in charge snapped out orders and several uniformed men prepared to rush the building. But the frenzied activity came to a sudden stop when the police phone rang.

For a moment everyone froze. And then, at the second ring, the commanding officer reached for the receiver. He listened for a moment, then nodded. "Okay. Sit tight. Help is on the way." He replaced the receiver and turned to the assembled group.

"Ruelas turned the gun on himself. Let's get a doctor up there on the double and move in. Johnson and Mitchell are okay."

Jess heard the words. Processed them. And then she did something she'd never done before.

She fainted.

Jess heard the voice calling her name from a long way off. The voice she'd been afraid she would never hear again. And as her eyelids flickered open and she saw the face that matched the voice, she knew the nightmare was over. Scott was safe.

"She's coming around."

At the sound of the unfamiliar voice, Jess transferred her gaze to a uniformed figure on her other side with a stethoscope around his neck. A paramedic. Only then did she realize that she was lying on the ground. "Did I faint?" she asked in surprise.

The worried frown on Scott's face eased and he squeezed her hand. "You've been out cold for ten minutes."

"The vitals all seem to be okay," the paramedic said. "How do you feel?"

Jess looked at Scott, and tears of relief flooded her eyes as she reached out to touch his weary face. "Grateful to have my husband back," she replied in a choked voice.

Scott covered her hand with his own, and their gazes locked in silent communication that spoke more eloquently than words of the love that filled their hearts.

"We can take you in and have you checked out just to be safe," the paramedic offered.

Jess's gaze never left Scott's. "I'm already safe," she said softly.

And as Scott reached for the woman he loved and tenderly took her in his arms, his heart overflowed with joy. For he knew that at long last he had truly come home.

Epilogue

"**Y**ou look beautiful. Don't touch a thing."

Jess set the comb back on the counter and slowly turned to Scott. She had never seen him look more handsome—even on their *first* wedding day. His dove-gray suit sat well on his broad shoulders, and his silver-and-maroon tie looked elegant against his starched white shirt. The silver flecks in his hair added a distinguished touch, and the fine lines in his face that had appeared over the past few years spoke of character and caring rather than age.

But it was his eyes that set her heart racing. Because they were the eyes of a man deeply, irrevocably in love—who was making no attempt to hide his love as his gaze moved leisurely, appreciatively over his wife.

"I like the dress."

Jess blushed and self-consciously smoothed a non-existent wrinkle out of the sleeveless, knee-length ivory lace sheath that flattered her slender figure. Though it had been hastily purchased, it was clear from Scott's expression that she'd made a good choice. "Thank you." She reached for the boutonniere that lay next to her bouquet. "Do you need some help with this?"

"Absolutely."

She stepped toward him and reached up to his lapel, all too aware of his almost tangible—and overpowering—virility. The distinctive, masculine scent of his aftershave filled her nostrils, and they were so close that his breath was a warm caress on her cheek. Suddenly she began to quiver. Not in fear, but in anticipation. For soon they would once again be man and wife in the fullest sense of the word.

It took her fumbling fingers several tries to secure the boutonniere, but at last it was firmly in place. She made a move to step back, but Scott grasped her upper arms and held her in place, forcing her to meet his eyes. His gaze searched hers, incisive, assessing. "Any second thoughts?" he asked.

She looked at him steadily and shook her head. "None."

He studied her for a moment longer, as if to reassure himself, then lowered his head to claim her lips in a lingering kiss that was filled with passion and promise.

"No more of that until *after* you renew your vows," a voice interrupted teasingly.

Scott and Jess turned to find Reverend Young in the doorway, and Scott grinned. "Then let's get this show on the road."

The minister chuckled. "My sentiments exactly. I'll meet you in the gazebo."

Scott retrieved Jess's bouquet, then reached for her hand and laced his fingers with hers. "Ready?"

She smiled, and when she spoke her voice was quiet but confident. "Yes."

With an encouraging squeeze of her hand, Scott led her outside. And as they began their walk through the garden he had so lovingly created, she thought about her answer. Yes, she was ready. Ready to let go of the past. Ready to move forward, into the future, with the man she loved. Ready to touch the sky.

Scott, too, was ready. To start a new chapter of his life with the woman he cherished. And he was glad they'd chosen to begin this way. Though their marriage had never actually ended, he and Jess had felt that it needed an official new beginning. And they'd wanted to share this moment with the people who meant so much to them.

As they walked down the path toward the gazebo, he let his gaze travel over the group assembled by the lake. Karen and her family were there, and even from a distance he could tell that his sister, always a sucker for happy endings, was already misty-eyed. Seth had come as well, looking slightly uncomfortable—but remarkably distinguished—in a suit. And Mark was there, grinning from ear to ear, clearly elated that his sister had at last taken his advice. Even Jess's parents had come. It had been touch and go with her father until the last minute, but in the end his love for Jess had outweighed his feelings about her husband. Scott knew he still had fence-mending to do with Jess's father, but he took Frank's presence today as a hopeful sign.

When they reached the gazebo and stepped up to join Reverend Young, Scott glanced down at Jess. Their gazes met and held, and her eyes reflected what was in his heart—gratitude for this second chance at love, and absolute trust that the Lord who had brought them back together would continue to stand by them and give them the strength and courage to face whatever challenges might lie ahead. And in that moment of silent communion their hearts pledged what words would reconfirm in just a few moments.

Reverend Young began to speak, and as Scott transferred his gaze to the minister he was filled with a feeling of absolute peace and completeness. For he and Jess had now come full circle. They'd survived the dark, bleak winter of pain and separation and loss. Now they stood poised on the threshold of a new day, a new season, one filled with the promise of hope and joy and love.

And as he and Jess prepared to renew their vows before God and their families and friends, he suddenly recalled the words Seth had said to him the first time they met. And he knew that they were true.

Spring always comes.

* * * * *

Dear Reader,

As this book goes to press, my parents are celebrating their forty-eighth anniversary. What an accomplishment in a world where half of marriages end in divorce. And what a shining example of the enduring power of love! Through good times and bad, in sickness and in health, they have faced life together, always knowing that their love would see them through.

In comparison to their forty-eight-year union, my marriage is a mere child at twelve years. But I already have a sense of how tough it can be to keep that "for better, for worse" vow. So many things take a toll on marriage. Demanding careers that leave couples little time—or energy—for each other. Unexpected disappointments that change the direction of your life together. Well-laid plans that go awry. Hurts that only time and a change of heart can heal.

Fortunately, few marriages have to overcome the kind of tragedy that Jess and Scott face in *Never Say Goodbye*. Instead, most are simply worn down by the petty annoyances of daily life. And in a world of "I-have-to-take-care-of-myself-first" attitudes and values that change from situation to situation, there is little to encourage the stick-to-it-iveness that is the glue of marriage. It's easier to just give up when trials and tribulations replace romance and roses.

But what a loss that is. Because it's the enduring power of love that gives marriage its depth and dimension. For there is incredible peace and joy in knowing that whatever happens, you'll still be together. And that your love will burn with an unquenchable flame that is steady and sure and strong all the days of your life. Just as my parents' has for nearly half a century.

Happy anniversary, Mom and Dad. I love you. Always.

Irene Hannon

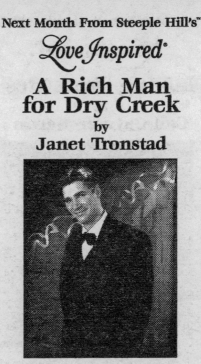

Next Month From Steeple Hill's

Love Inspired

Wedding Bell Blues
by
Cynthia Rutledge

David Warner needed a bride, and finding
Christy Fairchild after ten years seemed to be a good
sign. The love-wary businessman couldn't help but be
swept up by feelings from long ago, but could he trust
that the emotions they shared were blessed from above?

**Don't miss
WEDDING BELL BLUES**

On sale July 2002

Visit us at www.steeplehill.com

LIWBB